## "Look... Jack :

Anger and indignation slowly pulsed through Maddie. What right did he—a perfect stranger—have to question her feelings for Lamar? Did he think because they were mildly attracted to each other that he could demand to know her every secret? "You want the truth?" she snapped.

"That's all I've ever wanted."

She stared into his eyes, her gaze unwavering. "Then here's the truth," she said in a calm, even voice. "Lamar means more to me than any man I'll ever know. I'll love him forever. And I could never...ever...do anything that would hurt him." She paused. "Are you satisfied?"

"There's only one thing that will satisfy me," Jack murmured, his gaze skimming over her face to rest on her lips.

"And what is that? Please tell me. I'd be happy to oblige."

"This," Jack murmured. He grabbed her arms, his hands hot on her bare flesh, and pulled her against him. She drew in a sharp gasp, but the sound of the pulse pounding in her temples obliterated everything else.

Jack lowered his head until his mouth was nearly on hers. "Lamar's gone, Maddie." He drew in a deep breath. "But I'm here. And God help me, I want you...."

Dear Reader,

All right, I'll be the first to admit it. I fall in love with my heroes. How can a writer keep from losing a little bit of her heart to a man she's created herself?

When my editor approached me about doing a book in the HERO FOR HIRE series, I immediately saw all the possibilities. Here was a chance to create a modern-day Knight in Shining Armor, a man who'd give his life to protect the Damsel in Distress. He'd be everything I'd ever fantasized a hero to be—charming, witty, incredibly handsome and sexy. And just a tad arrogant. In walked Jackson Beaumont, the younger brother of my hero in *Love Potion #9*.

I couldn't offer Jackson Beaumont and Madeline Delaney an ordinary story. So I gave Jack a dead body to guard and Maddie a body to die for. I tossed in a little mystery, a sultry Louisiana setting and a lot of crazy characters. And I ended up with a book that was completely different from anything I'd ever written before.

Except…one thing was the same. By the time I typed The End, I'd fallen in love with Jack Beaumont. I hope you will, too.

Happy reading!

Kate Hoffmann

# A BODY TO DIE FOR
## *Kate Hoffmann*

A BODY TO DIE FOR

**HARLEQUIN**®

TORONTO • NEW YORK • LONDON
AMSTERDAM • PARIS • SYDNEY • HAMBURG
STOCKHOLM • ATHENS • TOKYO • MILAN • MADRID
PRAGUE • WARSAW • BUDAPEST • AUCKLAND

For Audra Kristine.
My sunshine on a rainy day.

ISBN 0-373-25797-X

A BODY TO DIE FOR

Copyright © 1998 by Peggy Hoffmann.

This edition published by arrangement with Harlequin Books S.A.

® and TM are trademarks of the publisher. Trademarks indicated with
® are registered in the United States Patent and Trademark Office, the
Canadian Trade Marks Office and in other countries.

**Printed in U.S.A.**

# _____ Prologue _____

JACKSON BEAUMONT considered himself a connoisseur of the female form. From the time he was ten, when he'd first noticed girls were more fun to look at than cars and boats, he'd made it his business to appreciate the endless fascination a woman's body provided.

Unlike many men, he chose not to limit his diet, and instead partook of the full range of feminine pulchritude—willowy blondes, curvacious brunettes, fiery-tempered redheads. At one time or another in his life, he'd taken pleasure in each and every one. But as he stood outside Mark Spenser's office, staring at the woman within, he sensed that here was a new and unique dish.

She was dressed entirely in black, from her wide-brimmed hat to her sexy "seduce me" high heels. He couldn't see her face, hidden behind a swath of black net, but he did have a fine view of her legs—long, slender, shapely limbs crossed primly at the knee and encased in black-seamed silk. His eyes followed the dark line that traced a path from her heel, to her calf, disappearing behind the sweet bend of her knee.

"The Black Widow."

Jackson glanced over his shoulder at Jon Wilcox, the flamboyant boyfriend of general manager Mark Spenser. "She's a widow?"

Jon nodded, then sighed dramatically. "She certainly has the drama down. Bette Davis wore a suit just like that in *All About Eve*. Marilyn was in that movie, you know. And I'd give up a kidney for that hat. I've always had a weakness for veils. Sunshine did my reading the other day and said I was Scarlett O'Hara in another life."

Jack laughed and shook his head. Sunshine Seagull, a flower child well past her "childhood," ran the Fifth Dimension Tea Shop down the street and provided Jon's daily dose of New Age Wisdom. "You were a fictional character in another life?"

Jon waved his hand. "I know, I know."

Of all the people that wandered through the front doors of the S. J. Spade "Insurance Agency," Jon Wilcox was by far the most colorful. An aspiring chef and part-time drag queen, Jon usually appeared around lunchtime with one of his creations for Mark and the office staff to sample. Each dish was named for Marilyn Monroe, Jon's idol and alter ego. Today it had been hors d'oeuvres—"Some Like It Hot" chicken wings and "Gentlemen Prefer Brie" baked cheese, topped with weird vegetables, in some kind of pastry thing.

"Sunshine says fiction is merely another plane of reality," Jon continued. "But I do have this undeniable urge to dress up in my mama's portiers."

"Portiers?" Jack asked, raising an eyebrow. "Let me guess. Some kind of exotic ladies' underwear?"

"Oh, this is choice," he said. "The smooth and suave Jack Beaumont asking me about ladies' underwear." Jon clucked his tongue and shook his head. "They're drapes, you rube. You know, curtains. Window treatments?"

Jack frowned, the train of conversation completely lost on him now. "I thought you wore dresses."

"Hello! Ever hear of a little film called *Gone With The Wind?* Scarlett, Rhett? And that divine Ashley?" He groaned. "Rent the movie and then we'll talk, Beaumont."

As Jon walked away, mumbling to himself, Mark Spenser stepped out of S. J. Spade's office down the hall, a file folder in his hand. From his conservative dress and efficient nature, it was hard to believe he and Jon had anything in common. But then, inside the Victorian row house overlooking San Francisco's Golden Gate Bridge, nothing was really as it seemed.

Very few citizens of San Francisco knew that behind the facade of the S. J. Spade Insurance Agency lurked a successful fifteen-year-old business that provided bodyguard services for anyone willing to pay for protection. And though Samantha Spade's reputation was impeccable, to Jack's knowledge, none of the employees had set eyes on her—except for Mark.

"I was just speaking with Samantha," Mark said, glancing at his watch. "Even though you've only been with the agency a month—"

"Two months," Jack corrected.

"Seven weeks," Mark countered. "Even so, she's confident you're ready to handle this case."

He handed Jack the file and Jack's eyebrows rose in surprise. "I get the Black Widow?"

Mark shook his head impatiently. "Mrs. Parmentier to you."

Jack opened the file. "So, what's this all about?" Since he had come on board, he'd been assigned most of the scut work, even though his previous job experience made him one of the most highly trained members of the staff. But Mark was adamant—Samantha Spade expected him to pay his dues like everyone else. So Jack had grudgingly guarded his share of would-be movie stars, brooding businessmen, mouthy ex-athletes and even a few pampered pets. Any hour of the day or night, he was on call, ready to jump in the car or hop a plane for the next job.

"Samantha will give you the details," Mark said. "She's waiting on line two so you'd better get your butt in there."

Jack smiled to himself and tapped the file against his hip. Finally, it looked like he was about to get a case that would prove more intriguing than the rest...especially if it involved guarding the lady in black.

He stepped into Mark's office and smiled at his newest client. "Mrs. Parmentier." Her name stumbled off his tongue as he tried to match Mark's exacting pronunciation, *Pah-men-tee-ay*. "I'm Jackson Beaumont. I'll be handling your case." He held out his hand, and the woman slowly rose from her seat, turning her gaze in his direction.

She stared at him for a long moment, then took his hand, her black kid glove soft against his palm. He could just make out her features, blurred by the veil. High cheekbones, full red lips, wide, long-lashed eyes... A well-kept lady, he was sure, of indeterminate age. He'd guess maybe early forties.

A faint smile touched her lips. "Madeline Parmentier," the woman said. "Mr. Beaumont, it is a pleasure, diminished only by the circumstances that have brought me here."

A simple word, *pleasure* softly spoken, yet laced with an air of seduction. An experienced woman, Jack mused. She might have said "kiss me" or "take me" and he wouldn't have noticed any difference. The Old South infused her low voice like the scent of gardenias on a muggy afternoon, and he let it sink into his senses for a long, silent moment.

Mark cleared his throat, and Jack glanced back to

see him still standing by the door. He pointed to the phone, then his watch. With an apologetic smile, Jack reached over the desk and punched the button for the speaker phone.

"Morning, S.J.," he said. "Beaumont here."

"Jack! Sweetheart! Have you been introduced?"

Jack looked over at Madeline Parmentier, then back at the phone. "All done."

"Good," Samantha said. "Here's the scoop. Mrs. Parmentier's late husband, Judge Lamar Parmentier, was a former client of ours. We guarded a witness in an organized crime case he was presiding over. A boatload of wise guys took a little trip up the river after that one. And now Mrs. Parmentier needs our help."

"I'm certain we'll be able to do whatever is necessary to protect her." Jack gave Madeline Parmentier a reassuring smile, but she quickly dropped her gaze to her lap and took up a careful study of her gloves.

"All the dope's in the file. Charilyn is arranging for your plane ticket," Samantha continued. "You'll have just enough time to go home and pack a bag."

"Where am I going?" Jack asked.

"Louisiana," Samantha said.

"Fells Crossing," Madeline Parmentier added in a soft drawl. "Near Baton Rouge."

"Well, if there aren't any questions, Jack, I'm putting Mrs. Parmentier in your care."

"No problem," Jack said. "You can trust me to get the job done."

"You're an angel."

"Back at you," Jack replied. He listened as Samantha hung up the phone on the other end.

At the sharp click, Madeline Parmentier quickly stood, then smoothed her skirt. "I understand we'll be on the same flight to New Orleans, Mr. Beaumont. I've arranged for a driver to pick us up at the airport. I'll see you at the gate, then."

She turned toward the door, but Jack reached out and touched her elbow to stop her. A warm tingle shot up his arm and he did his best to rationalize it. So he hadn't touched a woman for a few months. He was new in town, he'd been working hard. "Mrs. Parmentier, if you're in danger, I think I should accompany you back —"

She glanced down at the place where his fingers rested on her arm, waiting until he pulled his hand away. "I'm in no danger, Mr. Beaumont," she finally said, then walked out the door.

Jack stared after her, a frown creasing his forehead. "Then why do you need a bodyguard?" he muttered to no one but himself.

He was still standing in the middle of the office when Mark returned, plane ticket in hand. "Your flight's in two hours. Here's your cell phone and your company credit card. And don't forget your weapon this time. Expenses are to be related directly to the case and not to be used on whatever floozy you find to occupy your free time."

"Floozy?"

Mark shook his head. "You and Lucas Kincaid. Sex, boats and rock 'n' roll. Speak of the devil, you got a postcard from him." Mark held it out, and Jack snatched it from his fingers. "Behave yourself, Beaumont," Mark warned. "And as Samantha would say, keep your paws off the dame."

Jack chuckled. "Don't get your boxers in a knot, Spenser," he teased. "I'm one of the good guys. I'm not about to pull a Kincaid here and run off with one of the clients. You can trust me on this."

"Yeah, right," Mark muttered, retreating into his office.

Jack glanced down at the postcard, a picture of whales, then read the note on the back. "Having a great time. Glad you're not here. *Hoo-ah*, Kincaid."

Lucas had found the girl of his dreams, a pretty lady named Grace. Jack flipped the card back over and stared at the photo. His buddy was married by now and probably on his way to another exotic port of call.

Jack sighed. Lucas Kincaid was the last person he'd have pegged to settle down. But then even the toughest guys stepped off the plank sooner or later. Jack shoved the postcard in his back pocket. "Not me," he murmured, heading toward the front door. "Not in a million years. I gave up on that whole fairy tale a long time ago."

## 1

THE AIR-CONDITIONING in the car barely made a dent in the heat of the Louisiana afternoon. Jack felt a trickle of sweat slide down his spine, and he squirmed in his seat. The pavement of the interstate wavered at the horizon and the lush green trees on either side were coated with the dust of a late summer's day. He stared out the car window and tried to appreciate the landscape. But his mind continually returned to the cool and composed woman sitting next to him in the back seat of the old Bentley sedan.

He glanced over at Madeline Parmentier. Like him, she'd chosen to focus on the scenery flying past the windows, her veiled face averted from his side of the car. He had to admit that from his point of view, the scenery inside the car was much more interesting.

His gaze covertly scanned the length of her body, coming to rest on her ankles, neatly crossed one over the other. The black seams in her silk stockings beckoned enticingly. How had men managed to keep their heads, back when all ladies' stockings had had seams? As far as he was concerned, that little black seam was like a road map right into the bedroom.

He couldn't even bear to consider what might be holding those stockings up. A black lace garter belt with those little satin roses? Maybe some ribbon tossed in? Something right out of those catalogs he and the guys on his SEAL teams used to pass around when they got bored—or lonely. Jack sighed inwardly. He'd do better to occupy his attention with the safety of his client and not the selection of her underwear.

Maybe that was the problem—he wasn't really cut out for this bodyguard business. The way Jack saw it, this was all just a waiting game, and he'd never been one to sit around and wait for something to happen. In the SEALs, he and Lucas Kincaid and the rest of their team took action—quick and decisive action that kept them on the offensive. But a bodyguard was all about defense, and Jack Beaumont didn't like being on the defensive.

Still, he could think of worse things than sitting around watching Madeline Parmentier. He hadn't gotten a good look at her face yet, but a woman with legs like hers was bound to be beautiful. And though she might be a bit older than the women he usually found himself attracted to, so what? A gorgeous woman was a gorgeous woman.

Jack turned back to the window. Was that what Lucas Kincaid had thought before he got caught up with a client and ended up married? Jack had first met Lucas Kincaid at Annapolis, when Lucas was a plebe with a serious attitude and Jack had been his battalion commander. They'd met again four years later when Kincaid was assigned to Jack's SEAL team as the newest "new guy." For four months, the team gave him hell, until the next "new guy" arrived.

Their friendship really blossomed the night Kincaid stepped up and helped Jack out in a bar fight, fracturing his own jaw in the process. From then on, they'd been tight. Best friends on and off the job. When Kincaid had been caught in a mission gone bad and imprisoned in a Caribbean hellhole, Jack had been the first one to volunteer for the "liberation" team.

But freeing Lucas Kincaid had taken its toll. It had left Lucas burned out and eager to resign from the team and from the navy. And it had left Jack with an injury to his knee that put him out of the SEALs for good. He'd been offered an assignment in "intel" and had spent an endless year there, pushing paper, before finally following his friend into civilian life.

The first nine months he had knocked around San Diego, ferrying sailboats up and down the Pacific coast for wealthy clients, living from day to day, never knowing where the next job or the next paycheck would come from. For a while, he'd even thought about returning to Baltimore and repairing the mess he'd made with his family—his two brothers in particular.

But then Kincaid had called and urged him to apply for a job with S. J. Spade. Jack had jumped at the chance, anxious to work with his old buddy again. Hell, if Lucas could put up with a regular job, so could he. But Jack hadn't realized the position he was offered was the same one vacated by his best friend.

Still, a job was a job. And on the Beaumont scale of adventure, bodyguarding seemed to offer the most potential for action. Though he could have tried life as a cop or a fireman, Jack knew he was long past the point of taking orders from anyone. Once he was on a case with the Spade Agency, he pretty much ran the show, and he liked it that way.

So why wasn't he doing that now? Instead of staring out the window, he should be questioning Mrs. Parmentier, learning the details of her case. The file provided only the minimum information. He turned his head, his gaze falling on her legs once more, then bit back a soft moan.

"I was sorry to hear of your loss, Mrs. Parmentier," he said.

She faced him, her shoulders stiff. "My loss?"

"Your husband?"

"Oh," she replied. "Yes, my husband. Thank you."

"Why don't you tell me about your...situation? The death of your husband. Why do you need a body-guard?"

She slowly sat back in the leather seat and smoothed her skirt over her thighs, but he could feel her perusal from behind the veil. She didn't trust him, not by a long shot. "Beaumont," she murmured. "That name is familiar to me. Are you by chance related to the Tol-liver Beaumonts of New Orleans?"

A social climber, too? Jack shook his head. "No. I'm originally from Maryland. Baltimore, to be precise. I grew up on the Chesapeake."

"And have you ever guarded a body before, Mr. Beaumont?"

"I'm well qualified to protect you, Mrs. Parmentier. Before I joined the agency, I was in special ops with the navy. I'm highly trained in all levels of security. You have nothing to fear."

"I have no doubts about your physical abilities," she said, her gaze now skimming the length of *his* body. "What concerns me is your..." she tipped her head to the side, the veil lifting slightly to reveal the pale column of her neck, remarkably smooth for a woman of her age "...discretion."

Jack's eyes fixed on a spot at the base of her throat. He could almost imagine pressing his mouth right there, feeling her pulse beneath his lips, her warm, silken skin. Dragging his gaze away, he cleared his throat. "Discretion? I'm not sure what you mean."

"I live in a small town, Mr. Beaumont. My late husband was one of the town's most prominent citizens. A judge. He has—he *had* many friends and at least one enemy."

Jack's breath caught and his instincts, momentarily dulled by lust, turned razor sharp. Geez, a year off the teams and already he was getting soft in the head. "Are you saying Judge Parmentier's death wasn't from natural causes?"

She shifted and carefully folded her hands on her lap. As a SEAL, he'd been trained to look for "tells," those tiny tics and quirks that betrayed a person's real thoughts and motives. Beneath her gloves, he was certain he'd find white knuckles and sweaty palms. Madeline Parmentier was hiding something.

"We'll discuss my suspicions when we get back to Felicity," she replied, a very slight tremor detectable in her voice.

"Felicity?"

"The judge's family home near Baton Rouge. That's where we live—I mean, lived. I live there now. Alone."

"Mrs. Parmentier, if you believe your husband was murdered, you have to relay your suspicions to the authorities. Have you talked to them? And if you're afraid for your safety, why go back there? Why not wait until the matter is resolved with the police?"

"I have to go back," she replied, ignoring his first question. "I don't have a choice." She rose from her chair. "Mr. Beaumont, when we get back home, you're going to hear many things that might give you pause. I want you to remember that you're working for me.

I'll need your discretion—and your loyalty. I require it."

"And you'll have it. Unconditionally."

A soft sigh escaped her lips, fluttering the black veil. "Good."

She went back to watching the scenery, and Jack slowly realized that she didn't intend to reveal anything more. All right, he mused. For once in his life, he could wait. Sooner or later, he'd find out why she needed protection. And then he could finally concentrate on the job and get his mind off Madeline Parmentier's sexy legs.

"WHY DID YOU BRING that man here? I can see trouble comin' and you got the gate wide open, Maddie Delaney!"

Maddie tossed her purse on the ornately carved tester bed, then spun to face Calpurnia Winslow, Felicity's cook and housekeeper. The imperious black woman regarded her with a petulant expression, her hands hitched on her ample waist.

"I didn't have a choice," Maddie cried. "We needed help. Truett hasn't slept in three days! And we're all getting a little testy." She tugged off her gloves. "And call me Mrs. Parmentier! Madeline Parmentier."

She'd hidden behind that name since early this morning, and she wanted to toss it aside the same way she had her gloves and purse. Playing the part of the Widow Parmentier was a task that weighed too heavily on her shoulders. Everyone was depending on her to remain calm, to keep it all together, to make their plan work. But all Maddie wanted to do was crawl beneath the covers of the bed and hide.

There had been a time when she'd been adept at lies and deception. Her survival had depended upon it.

But that time had been long ago, in another life. All that was left to draw upon now was sheer determination, and in the face of Jack Beaumont's charm, her determination was wavering badly. She'd have to summon every bit of her resolve to get through the next week.

She would just have to do what she had to do. Wasn't that exactly how her life had always been? She didn't like to lie, didn't enjoy deceit. But when survival fell into the murky gray waters between right and wrong, she knew better than anyone how to navigate.

Maddie flopped into an overstuffed chair near the fireplace and kicked off her shoes, then looked around the bedroom. She was safe here, in familiar surroundings. She'd always loved this room, with its pale yellow walls and pretty, feminine furniture. It had belonged to the real Mrs. Parmentier, Lamar's treasured Sarah. Most of the pieces had been in the family since before the Civil War, purchased from the very best furniture makers in New Orleans, especially for the lady of the house.

But Maddie was lady of the house now. And she was expected to act the part. The grieving widow, pining after the man she had loved and lost. Oblivious to the disturbing attraction she felt toward a total stranger. She'd be indifferent and aloof, keeping all her doubts and insecurities buried so deep that Jack Beaumont would never see them.

Maddie groaned and rubbed her temples with her fingertips. "This is never going to work. I thought I'd get some guy with more brawn than brain. I didn't expect someone so...shrewd."

Calpurnia clucked her tongue. "You mean, easy on the eyes?"

"No," Maddie retorted. "I meant exactly what I said." She swallowed hard. "Intelligent. He's bound to figure out what we're up to. I should just send him back to where he came from. This was all a mistake."

"Send him back all suspicious? You got him here, little girl, now you're goin' to have to deal with him. Though I suspect you'll find yourself a way."

Maddie's eyebrow arched. "And what is that supposed to mean?"

"Look at yourself! All dressed up like some Saturday-night harlot. You could tell the man the moon was green and he'd probably believe you. A good-lookin' man in this house," she muttered. "An' you bein' a single woman with needs. It's trouble waitin' to happen."

Calpurnia always managed to cut right to the chase. Maddie had known Calpurnia and Truett Winslow for years. Calpurnia was the closest thing she had to a mother, and though her obstinate opinions and un-flinching honesty weren't always welcome, Maddie knew they came out of concern for her well-being. Still, she drew the line at Calpurnia's comments on her sex life—or the lack of one.

"I don't have needs," Maddie snapped, pushing out of the chair. "I never have."

"I wasn't born on Crazy Creek, so don' go tryin' to fool me. You aren't clever enough by half." Calpurnia flipped open Maddie's suitcase and began to sort through her clothes. "Every woman has needs. An' you're no different, missy. B'sides, how's it goin' to look? You, a pretty, young widow and him a...a stud biscuit."

"Stud muffin," Maddie corrected with a soft laugh, grabbing a silk scarf from Calpurnia's hand. She

couldn't have devised a more fitting description for
the handsome Mr. Beaumont.

Calpurnia snorted. "You're back in the heart of
Dixie, missy. We prefer biscuits to muffins. And we
also like our grievin' widows behavin' in a seemly
manner."

Maddie carefully folded the scarf and placed it in
the chiffonier near the window. "He *is* handsome,"
she murmured.

And tall. Broad shouldered and loose limbed. With
thick dark hair that seemed perpetually windblown.
And a charming dimple that only came out when he
smiled, which he seemed to do a lot when he looked at
her.

To be honest, she'd nearly groaned out loud when
he'd walked into the office and introduced himself.
She'd expected some burly Neanderthal with a slop-
ing forehead and massive biceps, a real knuckle drag-
ger. Instead, she found herself staring at a certified
Greek god, a charming man with a physique that
women drooled over—and a face to match. Perhaps
that's why she hadn't insisted on another bodyguard,
one with a lower IQ. She'd been temporarily blinded
by his good looks.

"I just have to figure out what to tell him," Maddie
said. "He thinks I hired him to guard me. If I tell him
the truth, he's probably going to want to go back to
San Francisco. That would solve all our problems.
Then I could go out and hire someone…dumber."

"You're payin' him, aren't you?" Calpurnia said.
"He'll stay."

"But all the money in the world might not be
enough," Maddie said hopefully.

Calpurnia snapped Maddie's suitcase shut and
hefted it over to the closet. "Well, he's your problem.

You just watch yourself, you hear me?'' she admonished. "We all have too much at stake here."

The woman bustled out of the room, heading down to the kitchen to begin dinner preparations. Maddie sat down on the edge of the bed and rubbed her tired eyes. They were counting on her to make this work. She couldn't make it work *with* Jackson Beaumont—and she couldn't make it work *without* him.

But could she keep up this charade? Beaumont was already asking too many questions. She'd managed to escape his office unscathed. And the flight had been passed with her safely installed in first class and Beaumont in coach. She had been dreading the ninety-minute ride from the airport, but she'd managed a short conversation without slipping up.

Like his wife, Calpurnia, Truett Winslow wasn't in favor of bringing a bodyguard back to Felicity. But though Truett was vigilant, he couldn't provide protection twenty-four hours a day. And they'd already learned that to rely on the rest of the staff would be foolhardy.

Emile, the judge's octogenarian driver, was so nearsighted that his regular duties had been reduced to washing and waxing the cars once a week. Luis, the gardener, was so obsessed with his flowers that he couldn't be dragged away from his job for more than a few hours each day. And Jim Bob, the stable boy, was just too young to depend on.

Along with Calpurnia and Truett, they were all part of the "scam" and had enthusiastically endorsed it. But she'd known from the start that she'd be the one under pressure to make the plan work. Now all she had to do was keep Jackson Beaumont in check.

Maddie stood up and wandered over to the tall French doors that opened from the bedroom onto the wide gallery. The scent of Luis's potted camellias drifted through the window on the heavy, humid air. Early September in Louisiana could be blazingly hot, and today was no exception.

Felicity was a beautiful old antebellum home with majestic columns that surrounded the two-story house and supported a well-shaded gallery. Gnarled live oaks, some nearly two hundred years old, dotted the property and lined the front drive. On either side of the house were formal gardens, roses dominating the east garden and azaleas to the west. Her bedroom overlooked the rose garden.

As she stepped outside for a breath of air, Maddie tugged out her hat pin and pulled off her hat, letting her shoulder-length hair tumble around her face. She tossed the hat on a wicker settee, then reached for the buttons at the neck of her fitted jacket.

"Mrs. Parmentier?"

The sound of a man's voice startled her, and she spun around to see Jack Beaumont watching her, his shoulder braced against one of the columns. Without the protection of her veil, she was forced to meet his surprised gaze squarely—and with more confidence than she actually had. She forced a smile. "Mr. Beaumont. I see you've discovered the relief our gallery offers. It's sometimes the only way to bear the summer heat."

He stared at her long and hard, scrutinizing her features with a shrewd eye. Maddie wasn't sure what she should do. Could he see the anxiety in her expression, read the apprehension in the nervous set of her jaw? Could she boldly lie to this man and get away with it? She had never been an adept actress, and their encounter in San Francisco had taken every ounce of concentration she possessed.

"Mr. Beaumont? Is there anything wrong?"

He blinked once before his expression softened. "I'm sorry. What did you say?"

"Your room. Is everything to your liking?"

"Yes," he murmured.

He stepped closer and she felt a shiver skitter along her spine in the cloying heat. "Is—is there something else I can do for you?"

He slipped between her and the railing, standing so close they nearly touched. He wanted something from her; she could sense it deep inside, where feminine instinct resided. He fixed his gaze on a spot over her shoulder. "Yes. You can go back inside. This veranda is too exposed and you're a soft target."

A soft target. Why did that sound like a compliment to her? "But I—"

Jack gently took her arm and led her back to her bedroom. "You hired me to protect you, Mrs. Parmentier," he said, his jaw tight. "I'm just doing my job."

Maddie shook her head. "I don't think you understand."

"I understand completely. It's my job to protect you."

A sigh escaped her lips. Avoiding the inevitable would only raise more questions, and the last thing she needed from Jack Beaumont was more of his infernal and incessant questions. "I didn't hire you to protect me," she said softly. "I hired you to protect my husband."

Jack stopped short, his firm grip pulling her to a halt in front of him. "I thought your husband was—"

"Please. Come with me." She led Jack through her bedroom to a door in the far wall. Pulling it open, she showed him into the parlor between her room and Jack's. In the center of the room, an ornate mahogany

coffin gleamed beneath the soft light from an electri-
fied antebellum chandelier. She nodded at the stable
boy, Jim Bob, and he hurried into the hallway, pulling
the door shut behind him.

"Mr. Beaumont, I'd like to present my late husband,
Judge Lamar Parmentier. He's the one you'll be
guarding."

Jack gasped, then snapped his gaze back to hers.
"You want me to guard a—a dead man?"

She focused her concentration once again, trying to
decide between a plausible lie and the dubious truth.
She could tell him it was Parmentier family tradition,
that there were always family members to sit vigil
with the dearly departed until burial. Had Jack been
from the Deep South, he surely would have believed
her story. There were plenty of odd traditions associ-
ated with every important event from birth to death.
Keeping a corpse company ranked rather low on the
oddity scale.

Or she could tell him the truth. That Judge Lamar
Parmentier needed protection more than she did.
"Yes, Mr. Beaumont. I want you to guard my hus-
band."

"I—I'm just supposed to sit here with the coffin?"

Maddie shrugged. "I suppose you could speak if
you'd like. We believe the departed take comfort in
having a mortal companion nearby as they make their
way to their great reward."

A scowl hardened his features and Maddie knew
that he wasn't pleased with his duties. She drew a
deep breath. If this was going to work, she had to have
Jack Beaumont on her side. And looking at him now,
she knew that it would take more than just a paycheck
to keep him on the job. It would take the truth, at least

that portion of the truth she was willing to reveal to him.

"When I mentioned my husband's death," she began slowly, "I didn't tell you the whole story. I *have* contacted the authorities and related my suspicions. You see, in the two weeks prior to Lamar's unfortunate demise, there were several incidents that appeared to be accidents. But looking back now, I can see they may have been attempts on his life. There was a stray shot while he was hunting and then a broken strap on his saddle."

"How did he die?"

"It appears to have been a heart attack, although Sheriff Dilby believes it could have been poison."

"How?"

"The judge always enjoyed a brandy after dinner. Usually Truett pours for him and leaves the glass on the judge's desk. That night, he did as he usually did. We believe someone came in through the open French doors and…" She let her voice drift off. "There was never a reason to have concern for his safety."

"Don't you think it's a little late to call me in?" Jack asked.

"Fells Crossing is a small Southern town, Mr. Beaumont. Rumors fly…speculation runs rampant. Sheriff Dilby has heard tell there are doubts about Lamar's death, that some folks have…" she paused for effect "…seen him around town. After consulting with the sheriff, we've decided to use the rumors to our advantage. We're hoping that the murderer will come back to see if he's done the job right and proper. And to do that, he'll have to open that coffin."

"And that's where I come in," Jack finished.

"I'm afraid our local police force consists of Dilby and his part-time deputy. That's why I hired you."

"What about an autopsy? What poison was used? And where does the investigation stand? Does Dilby have any suspects?"

Maddie shook her head. So damn many questions! Why couldn't she have found a bodyguard with feathers for brains? "There was no autopsy. It was... against the judge's beliefs." She said a silent prayer that her answers sounded plausible. To her ears, they sounded downright ridiculous.

"But it would give you the cause of death—and a starting point for an investigation."

Maddie cleared her throat and stiffened her spine, trying hard to affect an icy composure. "My husband is dead, Mr. Beaumont. That's all that matters in the end."

"But—"

Maddie warned him off, raising her hand and fixing a properly pained expression on her face. "Please. This talk upsets me. I—I ..." She sighed for dramatic effect. "I can't speak of it." She tried to muster a few tears or watery eyes. She'd even settle for a runny nose, but to no avail. All she managed was a wrinkled forehead.

Jack placed his warm palms on her upper arms and gazed down at her. "I'm sorry. I didn't mean to—"

"Rest assured, Sheriff Dilby will do his part. I hired you to watch over my husband's earthly remains. Nothing more. Sheriff Dilby will take care of the rest."

Jack nodded, his jaw tight. "Not a problem. I can do that." He glanced over at the coffin, then back to her. "I assume I've got the night watch."

"Ten until five. Jim Bob will complete the evening watch. We leave the doors unlocked and candles lit, just in case..."

"The murderer returns?"

Maddie nodded, then pressed her palms together. "If that's all for now, Mr. Beaumont, I need to help Calpurnia with dinner preparations. I dine at seven. I hope you'll join me."

He smiled. "If we're going to be dining together, I think you could call me Jack."

It was so much easier to call him Mr. Beaumont, Maddie mused. To maintain a polite distance. She could lie to Mr. Beaumont, but could she lie to Jack? Tall, gorgeous Jack with the quick smile and the clever eyes and irresistible dimple. There was no way to refuse his offer without sounding like a supercilious shrew. "All right...Jack. I'll see you at dinner."

"Until then, I'd like to take a closer look around the property, if you don't mind."

"No, I don't mind," Maddie replied, happy to have him out of the house and out of visual range. "Truett will show you the rest of the house and Luis knows the grounds better than anyone."

Relieved that she'd managed at least a modicum of calm, Maddie decided to make her escape. She hurried to the door, then turned, realizing that her departure seemed a little abrupt. "Calpurnia needs me in the kitchen," she muttered. "It's catfish and hush puppies tonight. If I don't watch her she'll fry the kitchen sink in lard and serve it up. I—I'll see you at dinner."

He smiled that smile again. The one that melted her insides. "Until dinner then," he said.

SHE WAS MORE BEAUTIFUL than he'd ever expected. When she'd been hidden behind the veil, he'd imagined someone much older, much...colder. The kind of woman who would marry an old man for money and prestige, then take secret relief in his death and in the prospect of spending the balance of his bank account on designer clothes and flashy jewelry. A stereotypical image of the younger widow, Jack had to admit, and one that vanished the moment he looked into Madeline Parmentier's soft green eyes. Hell, she wasn't much older than thirty, if she was a day.

Jack crossed his arms over his chest and watched from the shadows of the butler's pantry as she moved efficiently around the kitchen, the flowing skirt of her pretty summer dress nearly reaching her bare feet, a dish towel wrapped around her tiny waist. Her dark hair fell in damp tendrils from a haphazard knot on top of her head, and his fingers twitched with the urge to brush the strands from her nape and temples.

No, there was nothing mercenary there, nothing to disprove the notion that she'd truly loved a man old enough to be her grandfather. What he saw was a study in contrasts, vulnerability tempered by steely control, innocence mixed with a worldly attitude. But there was something else, something not quite right about Madeline Parmentier. He just couldn't put his finger on it.

He'd wandered into the dining room promptly at seven, only to find it empty, the long mahogany table set for two with china and silver, the beeswax candles in the huge candelabra lit and throwing a soft glow over the antique furnishings. The French doors had been thrown open to catch the evening breeze, fluttering the flames. But Madeline had been nowhere to be found. Then he'd heard voices coming from behind a tall door in a corner of the room, a door that lead to a cabinet-lined room off the kitchen. As he stepped into the butler's pantry, he had been assailed with incredible odors that set his mouth to watering—spicy, piquant, savory.

Since he'd arrived at Felicity, his senses had been assaulted again and again. The sweet smell of flowers hanging in the humid air. The sound of jays calling from the heavy boughs of the live oaks. The incredible beauty of Madeline Parmentier—her silky hair, liquid green eyes, lush lips. And now the scents coming from the kitchen. They all combined to overwhelm him, to muddle his senses and distract his mind.

"Vegetable oil," Madeline said, drawing Jack's attention back to the present. "Canola oil would be the best."

"I fry my hush puppies in lard," Calpurnia replied, a stubborn set to her jaw. "Makes 'em light and tasty."

Jack had met Calpurnia Winslow, Felicity's cook and housekeeper, on Truett's ten-cent tour. She didn't make an effort to hide her obvious distrust of him. In truth, she'd barely been civil. At least Truett managed a few polite replies to his questions, but Calpurnia just glowered, her dark eyes as dangerous as the cleaver she had wielded while decapitating fresh catfish.

"Never mind that they're fried, but do you have any idea what lard can do to a person's health? The FDA should outlaw it!"

"The judge likes his catfish and puppies the way I make 'em. I haven't heard any complaints lately."

Jack frowned. Considering the judge wasn't going to be eating much, Calpurnia's obstinacy seemed a bit out of line. Madeline Parmentier was her boss now, and should be obeyed. But then, Calpurnia was the type who took complete charge of her surroundings, including her beautiful mistress.

"The judge doesn't know what's good for him," Madeline replied, grabbing a bottle of oil and shaking it in the cook's direction. "As long as I'm in this house, we're going to eat healthier. No more lard!"

Calpurnia took a step toward Madeline, shaking her

finger. "You've got a low eye for a high fence when it comes to your cookin', missy," she said. "My gumbo is far-gone the best in Feliciana Parish, and when folks push back from my étouffée, they're just about as pleased as a basketful of possum heads."

"Just try the vegetable oil, Calpurnia. For Lamar's sake."

The cook carefully placed the crispy golden catfish on three plates, then arranged hush puppies and greens next to the fish. "Grab the hot sauce from the refrigerator," she said. "The judge likes hot sauce with his puppies. I'll finish making up his plate."

His plate? Jack frowned, then stepped into the kitchen. Surely they didn't plan to feed catfish to a corpse! His mind flashed an image of *Psycho*, of all those old horror movies and the wild-eyed inhabitants of creepy old houses. He and his brothers used to love those movies. He coughed softly. "Is dinner nearly ready?"

Madeline and Calpurnia spun around, their jaws dropping in tandem. The bottle of oil bounced on the floor and Calpurnia twisted her hands in her apron, darting a nervous look in Madeline's direction.

"How long have you been...waiting there, Mr. Beaumont?"

Eavesdropping was what she meant to say. Or maybe snooping. He stared at the plate Calpurnia was arranging. "You still make dinner for the judge?" he asked.

"I—I'm afraid you've misunderstood, Mr. Beaumont," Madeline stammered. "We were just reminiscing—about the judge's favorite dishes."

"Yes, indeed," Calpurnia added. "Why, sometimes we plumb forget he's gone and we make up a plate for him. Habit is hard to break, I suppose."

Madeline shot the cook a censorious glare, then scooped up two plates and brushed past Jack. "Dinner is served," she said.

With a tiny grin, Calpurnia looked at the third plate, then picked it up and followed. "Catfish and hush puppies," she muttered. "Fried in lard. The judge's favorite."

Jack stared after them as they hurried into the dining room. Sitting watch over a dead body was one thing, but setting a place for that body at the dining room table was on the other side of crazy. If they brought the corpse down and put in a chair, he was definitely going back to San Francisco! "I wanted an interesting case," he muttered. "Not bizarre, not peculiar. Just interesting."

By the time Jack stepped into the dining room, Madeline was already seated. Calpurnia stood behind the carved chair at the head of the table, and as Jack moved toward it, she pointed to a spot across from Madeline. "The judge sits at the head of the table. This is his spot. That's yours."

Feeling like a scolded schoolboy, Jack settled himself and reached for his linen napkin. Calpurnia dropped a plate in front of him, the glorious scent wafting up around him as she walked out of the room. "Looks good," he said.

"I know you must think we're a little…unusual," Madeline ventured, picking up her fork.

He couldn't help but smile. She looked so insecure, so unsure, as if she owed him an explanation for her behavior. "No, I don't think you're crazy."

She blinked in surprise at his alternate choice of description. "Well, we are," she said with a soft laugh. "I mean, look at us. A couple of betsy bugs. Setting a spot for Lamar as if he's going to walk in any moment, when we both know he won't."

Her light manner seemed forced. "Mrs. Parmentier, everyone handles grief in their own way."

"Maddie," she murmured, stabbing a hush puppy with her fork. "You might as well call me Maddie. Everyone else does. The judge calls—called me Madeline."

"Did you know the judge for a long time?" Jack asked, hoping to start a conversation that lasted more than a minute.

She paused, as if she wasn't sure about her answer. It was an easy question, Jack mused; a simple statement of fact would do. A year, a few months, a day or two. Why was she so hesitant to open up?

"It seemed like forever," Maddie said. "He was a kind man. He did a lot of good for people. For me." She nibbled on a piece of catfish. "Have you ever been married, Mr.—Jack?"

Jack smiled and popped a hush puppy in his mouth. The spicy dough melted on his tongue and he nearly groaned out loud. Calpurnia might be a prickly sort, but she sure knew her way around a kitchen. "How do you know I'm not married right now, Maddie?"

She cleared her throat nervously and glanced down at her plate. "Well, I suppose I don't. It's just that you don't wear a wedding ring."

"You looked?"

"No," she answered, tipping her chin up. "Well, just in passing. Besides, you don't act like a married man."

"And how is a married man supposed to act?"

She studied him for a long moment, her dark eyebrow raised. "A married man wouldn't stare at another woman's legs the way you were staring at mine in your office. And in the car."

So she'd noticed, Jack mused. "You do have nice legs, Maddie. Even the most loyal of husbands would be tempted. Especially by those black silk stockings with sexy seams running up the—"

"I believe I've made my point," Maddie interrupted. "Would you care for wine? This is a lovely chardonnay. It brings out the sweetness in the catfish." She filled his goblet and then her own.

Picking up his glass, he leaned back in his chair. For a woman who revealed very little of herself, she certainly was nosy about his personal life. Maybe that's what it would take to loosen her tongue a little. He'd reveal a few interesting bits about his past and she'd feel compelled to do the same. Besides, he'd reexamined his own personal history so many times, it had lost its ability to shock. And even if it did shock her, he'd enjoy watching that cool facade crack a little. "I was involved once," Jack offered.

Maddie glanced at him over the rim of her crystal goblet, curious now. "Involved? That's a vague word."

"We had a vague relationship. I dated Cynthia while I was going through airborne training, but it was nothing serious. At least, I didn't think so. I brought her home to meet the folks and she fell in love with my older brother, Jay. They got married, she got bored, and she showed up on my doorstep looking for some excitement."

Maddie took another sip of her wine in an attempt to hide her surprise, then carefully placed her glass on the table. "So...you had an affair with your brother's wife? That's either very audacious or very stupid, depending on the temperament of your brother."

Jack shrugged. "Cynthia was trouble, and I wasn't about to get mixed up with her again. But she told Jay that she never stopped loving me, that the only reason she married *him* was to force *my* hand. She also told him we were having an affair—while they were married. And he believed her. So you can see why I steer clear of permanent attachments."

"I—I suppose I can understand why," Maddie said.

"You can?"

A winsome smile curled the corners of her mouth. "It's easier to be alone," she said, choosing her words carefully. "There are no expectations, no demands, no confusion. No questions of trust or fidelity."

"Right," Jack continued. He had the strange feeling that she was talking about herself. "And you can do whatever you want, whenever you want—with whomever you want. And no one can stop you. Complete freedom."

"It's hard to live your life for someone else. Coming home to the same person night after night."

Jack set his own glass down. "But then, you married the judge, didn't you."

A slow blush crept up her cheeks. "I—I wasn't talking about myself," Maddie murmured. "I was talking about you. Besides, that all changes when you fall in love."

"And were you in love with the judge?"

"Of course I was."

Her answer came a little too quickly for his tastes. "Of course you were," he repeated, turning back to his dinner. But had she really been in love? He found it hard to believe that a woman like Maddie—a woman so beautiful, so sensual, so brimming with life— would be satisfied with marriage to an older man. But then, he really didn't know her at all.

That was going to change, however. He didn't plan to wait for Maddie to reveal herself—and her secrets. Before he left Felicity, he would learn all he could about the mysterious Widow Parmentier—and her dead husband.

## 2

THERE WERE TIMES when Maddie Delaney believed that food was a perfectly adequate substitute for sex. And for love, as well. But then, she hadn't experienced much of either in her thirty-three years. Maybe that's why she had become a chef. She found comfort in the kitchen.

Sure a girl couldn't warm her feet against a well-made béchamel or whisper passionately to a carefully finished beurre blanc, but Maddie felt something close to utter fulfillment when she perfected a recipe. She dipped a spoon into her saucepan and tasted the crawfish bisque she'd been working on since midnight. This was her fourth and last try, since Calpurnia would commandeer the kitchen in another hour for breakfast preparations.

Closing her eyes, Maddie let the velvety soup swirl over her tongue before she swallowed. "Oh, my," she said with a sigh. "I believe that's it." The perfect blend of sherry and cayenne left a tingle on her tongue, but didn't overwhelm the delicate taste of the crawfish or the sweetness of the fresh cream.

"Monsieur Aubert would have been proud." She'd mastered her roux years ago when she'd studied at the Cordon Bleu in Paris, study thanks in large part to the Lamar Parmentier Scholarship Fund for Juvenile Delinquents and Petty Criminals.

Every person at Felicity had benefited in some way

from the judge's gracious charity and undying faith in human nature. Maddie had met Lamar Parmentier when she was sixteen, and until then most everyone thought she was born tired and raised lazy. She'd left home—or what the social workers called her home— at the age of twelve, and never went back. There had been numerous stints in juvie for running away, for shoplifting and panhandling, for truancy and curfew violations.

There had been money to be made on the crowded streets of New Orleans' French Quarter, not with her body, which was too skinny to deserve any notice, but with her deft hands. The same hands that could dice an onion in seconds, whisk cream to an airy confection and open an egg with three fingers. She'd picked pockets along the Rue Bourbon, relieving tourists of their precious vacation cash.

The money had been good enough to keep her fed, and she'd managed to evade a stay in jail until she made the momentous mistake of picking the pocket of Judge Lamar Parmentier. Maddie smiled at the memory. She'd nearly made her getaway with his bulging wallet when she had felt his hand on the back of her neck.

But to her surprise, Lamar hadn't turned her over to the cops. Instead, he'd taken her into his town home in the fancy Garden District, cleaned her up and forced her to go to a strict parochial school in New Orleans. When she graduated, he'd helped find her a job in a famous French Quarter restaurant, where she watched and learned and bided her time. And when she was ready, he gave her the money to go to Paris and study cooking for two blissful years.

By the time she'd returned, she was a different person. Gone was the grimy pickpocket with the insolent attitude. She now dressed in the height of fashion and spoke fluent French. No one could touch her in the kitchen. But she still carried the scars of her youth, the insecurities and doubts, the need to hide her heart from those who might break it and shatter the dreams she'd held there for so long.

Lamar had picked her up from the airport that day seven years ago and had escorted her to a deserted building on a busy street in the Garden District. "This will be your new restaurant," he had told her. The rest was history. Within a few years, Delaney's had become as famous as Brennan's and K-Paul's and Commander's Palace, the interior patterned after a cozy Paris bistro.

"My regulars will love this bisque," she murmured, pulling the pan off the stove. "They'll *crave* this bisque. They'll have to have it once a week." Maddie made a few changes to the recipe in her notebook before she began to clean up the kitchen. But her task was interrupted when the kitchen door swung open.

Jack stood in the doorway, an empty coffee mug in his hand, his shirt unbuttoned to his waist. He stopped short when he saw her, then smiled. Why did it always seem like he was genuinely happy to see her? Maddie wondered.

"You're up early," he said, running his hand through his rumpled hair. "Or is it late? What time is it?"

He looked tired, Maddie mused, allowing her gaze to flit over his finely muscled chest. Perhaps she should have allowed him at least one night to settle in before assigning him guard duty. But the sooner he was sleeping his days away, the sooner he'd be out of her hair.

She forced a smile. Did she really want to avoid

him? Alone in the kitchen, she'd found herself returning again and again to thoughts of Jack Beaumont—his handsome face, his incredible body, his boyish smile and teasing blue eyes. Had she been on the lookout for a man, she might consider him a more than acceptable choice.

But she couldn't choose her men the way she chose fresh vegetables at the market. Though men might look good on the outside, might feel perfect to the touch and smell irresistible, they weren't like vegetables. They had a nasty habit of revealing their rotten insides once you got them home. She'd been with just enough men to know that for a fact.

No, she wasn't hungry for vegetables right now. Nor was she starving for male companionship. "It's four in the morning. And I haven't been to bed," Maddie said, wiping her hands on the dish towel tied around her waist. It was then she realized that she *had* been to bed. And she was still dressed in her nearly sheer silk nightgown and robe.

"What are you doing in here?" Jack asked.

She tossed the towel aside and retied her robe, pulling it tight over her chest. "Whenever I can't sleep, I cook," she explained. "Besides, Calpurnia doesn't allow me in her kitchen. I seem to interfere in her intimate relationship with lard."

"What are you making?"

"Crawfish bisque. Would you like to taste?"

Jack nodded and joined her at the stove. She dipped her spoon into the pot again, then held it up. Her breath caught when he covered her hand with his and maneuvered the spoon to his lips. Her gaze fastened on his mouth, on the tiny drop of cream that he caught with his tongue.

For a moment, she could have sworn he'd moved

closer. She imagined his eyes hooded, his mouth hovering near hers, the feel of his warm breath on his lips. Kissing him would be wonderful, the kind of experience that would send her senses reeling. He would taste like fine cognac, heady and pleasantly numbing.

"You're good," he said, a devilish grin quirking the corners of his mouth.

Maddie blinked, then looked from his mouth to his eyes. A challenging twinkle told her he knew exactly what she was thinking. With a silent curse, Maddie yanked the spoon from his grasp, spattering the leftover bisque into her face. Embarrassed, she reached for the towel, but Jack beat her to it. So much for swearing off vegetables.

"This is your kitchen," he said, carefully wiping her face. "You shouldn't have to sneak down here in the dead of night to cook."

"I told you, I—" His knuckles brushed her cheek, lingering for a long moment. She pulled back at the jolt of attraction that shot through her. Snatching the towel from his hand, Maddie turned back to the sink, gripping the edge until she regained her composure. "I couldn't sleep," she finished. She spun to face him. "Shouldn't you get back to the judge?"

"Truett is up. He asked if I'd make a fresh pot of coffee."

"I—I'll do it," Maddie said, grateful for the job. She hurriedly tossed chickory coffee into the filter and filled the pot with water. What was she doing, staring at Jackson Beaumont like some sex-starved teenager, praying that he'd kiss her? She touched her lips with her fingertips and brushed away the imaginary traces of her fantasies.

"Could I have some more of that?" Jack asked.

Maddie glanced over her shoulder. "What? More of what?"

Jack's eyebrow arched and Maddie felt a slow blush creep up her cheeks. "The crab soup. A guy can get a little hungry sitting around all night doing nothing."

Yes, the crab soup, she realized. What else would he be talking about? Certainly not the current of electricity that danced between them when he touched her! "It's bisque," she corrected, flipping the coffeepot on. "Crawfish bisque."

"Mud bugs," Jack said with a sleepy smile. "My brothers and I used to catch them and race them. But I never thought they could be used to make something so tasty."

"It's not the crawfish," Maddie said, scooping a ladleful of bisque into a bowl. "It's the chef." She put the bowl on the kitchen table, and Jack sat down and dug in. A moment later, she placed a basket of bread next to his place. "My latest attempt at baguettes. I'm still working on my mastery of yeast breads. I've never been much of a baker. But I'm an expert with sauces."

"This is really good," Jack said. "Better than Calpurnia's catfish and hush puppies."

"Do you think so?" Maddie asked. The thought that her cooking pleased him brought an odd sense of satisfaction. Though she'd had great reviews from all the critics, she'd always cooked to please her own tastes— until now. "It is good. The perfect balance, I think. So many chefs believe that more is better—more garlic, more cream, more butter. Sometimes more is just too much."

Her gaze fell again to his open shirt, to his smooth chest and the light dusting of hair, the warm, tanned skin. Well, maybe more didn't have to be too much. She fought the urge to push his shirt from his broad shoulders and clutched her fingers in front of her instead.

"You have a real passion for cooking, don't you?" he commented between bites, studying her with a curious eye.

"It's the only thing I truly do well," Maddie replied.

"I don't believe that. I'd imagine you do a lot of things well."

She shifted beneath his direct gaze. "It's true. I mean, I am a good cook."

"If I could find a woman who cooked as well as you," Jack teased, "I'd consider getting married, settling down."

Maddie felt another slow blush creep up her cheeks. Why did this man, and *only* this man, have the capacity to embarrass her so? "Would you like something to drink? Lemonade? A glass of wine?"

Jack nodded, pushing his bowl toward her. "Lemonade. And another bowl of sou—bisque."

She fetched both, then sat down beside him again. "You look tired. I'm sorry to put you on the night shift, but I didn't have much choice. Maybe we can work out a schedule where you won't have to stay up all night, every night."

*And then maybe I'll see more of you,* she mused. *Maybe I'll be able to figure out why you have such a disarming effect on me.*

"Actually, I got a little rack time." He glanced over at her. "Don't worry. In the SEALs we learn to sleep without really sleeping. The slightest sound brings me awake and alert."

Maddie let her breath out slowly. "Even so, I'll try to work out a schedule among you and Truett and maybe Luis."

"Speaking of Luis, I'd like to interview all of the

judge's employees. If you could get them together before lunch, I'd appreciate it."

She stiffened and pushed back from the table. "I thought I explained," she said, trying to keep her voice even. "I don't need you to do anything more than watch Lamar's coffin."

Jack's jaw tensed and his blue eyes lost their warmth. "Maddie, I'm here to do a job. And I'm going to do it the best way I can. That involves talking to everyone at Felicity. Someone killed your husband, and they're going to come back. How do you know it wasn't one of the staff?"

"No!" Maddie snapped, jumping up from her place at the table. "They loved Lamar. They'd never do anything to hurt him, believe me."

"You don't know that."

She began to pace between the table and the sink, frantic to regain control of this man, this situation. "Sheriff Dilby is doing all he can. He's quite competent. Just stay out of this!"

"Maddie, maybe you'd better sit down."

She raked her hands through her hair. "No. I'm tired and I need to get some sleep. I'm paying your fee, Mr. Beaumont. You'll do as I ask. If not, you can leave. I don't want you bothering the staff with your questions."

With that, Maddie turned and stalked out of the kitchen. When she reached the dining room, she placed her palms on the table and braced herself, drawing a deep breath. How much longer could she keep the true facts about Lamar's death from Jack?

Was she keeping these secrets to protect everyone at Felicity or had it become a way to protect herself? Playing the part of the grieving widow created a safe distance between her and Jack Beaumont. Whenever

he came too close, she could raise the mask and hide
behind her "despair."

She'd lived her life for her career, happy to put all
her energy and her passion into Delaney's. Why did
that have to change? Why did Jack Beaumont have to
come into her life and confuse everything?

Maddie shook her head. This was *all* her fault. She'd
invited him into her life, into this crazy scheme they'd
engineered. She'd opened the door and let him waltz
into Felicity. She'd just never expected to find him so
disarming...so attractive.

MADDIE SLEPT UNTIL NOON, exhaustion finally catching
up with her. The sun was high and the air thick with
midday heat when she walked down the stairs, her
shoes soft against the plush Oriental runner.

A small group had gathered around the library
door—Luis, still in his muddy coveralls and boots,
and Emile, dressed in his thirty-year-old chauffeur's
suit and hat. Jim Bob appeared from inside the library
moments later, a dandy brush clutched in his white-
knuckled hand.

"What's going on?" Maddie asked, her voice low,
her hand grasping the carved newel post.

Truett and Calpurnia stood at the center of the
group, concern etched deeply on their features. "He's
in there," Calpurnia whispered. "Woke himself up
around nine and demanded that we each see him in
the library."

"Why didn't you wake me?" she asked, hurrying
over to the library door. She pressed her ear against
the cool wood, but there was no sound coming from
within.

Calpurnia glared at her from beneath a beetled
brow. "He said you needed your rest. Seems to me

he's showin' a particular concern for your well-bein', missy."

"I'm sure that's only because I'm signing his paycheck," Maddie snapped, Calpurnia's words cutting too close. Jack was stubbornly doing his job, and he'd used every advantage, including her morning-long absence, to grill the inhabitants at Felicity. She'd warned him to stick to guarding the casket and he'd deliberately ignored her orders!

Luis sidled up to her. "What if he finds out the judge really didn't die the way we said he did?" he whispered.

"He won't," Maddie reassured the gardener.

"You shouldn't have brought him here," Calpurnia said.

Pressing the heels of her hands into her temples, Maddie moaned softly. "All right, perhaps I made a mistake. I just didn't think he'd be so nosy! But if I send him away now, he's going to be suspicious. We don't have much choice...unless we tell him the truth. The rest of the truth, that is."

"We could hit him over the head and bury him in the garden. He would make good fertilizer for my roses." Luis scratched his goatee. "Or maybe I should use him on the azaleas."

"I could accidentally run him over with the Bentley," Emile suggested, squinting through his tiny spectacles. "But Truett would have to accidentally knock him out in case I missed the first time."

Maddie shook her head. "For that matter, we could let Calpurnia's high-cholesterol diet do the dirty work. We are not going to bump off the bodyguard."

Jim Bob puffed out his chest. "But we could hurt him a little. I could lock him in the stall with Firebrand. That horse is a menace. A good kick in the noggin would change Beaumont's attitude."

She patted the boy on the shoulder. "Let's not worry until we have something to worry about. What did he ask? And what did you tell him?"

The quintet provided a brief rundown of Jack's questions and their answers. All of them were certain they hadn't let anything slip, that they had managed to act properly bereft at the judge's death and steadfastly loyal to his widow.

"Maybe this will satisfy him," Maddie said with a shrug. "Maybe he's finished asking questions." Though she tried to sound optimistic, she didn't hold out much hope on that front. Jack Beaumont was as tenacious as the kudzu that Luis did battle with in the garden. No matter how many times she thought she'd taken care of the problem, he kept coming back.

Calpurnia scowled. "I wouldn't give you a shovelful of chicken tracks on that bet."

"All right," Maddie said, frustration creeping into her voice. "What do you want me to do? The way I see it, I can send him back to San Francisco or I can tell him the truth. You decide."

Calpurnia hooked her thumb under her chin and pondered the problem. A wide smile slowly split her face. "Or you could tie a knot in his tail. Use your feminine wiles to distract the man. Dress yourself up and dab on a little perfume. Strut around in those floozy shoes you bought."

Eyes wide, Maddie gasped. She'd vowed to do whatever it took to protect those around her. But seduction was another matter entirely! "That is the craziest suggestion I've heard yet. Why, I'd just as soon have Luis whack him over the head with a garden shovel." She sent Luis a restraining look. "Why is it so important we keep this from him? What we've done isn't that bad. Maybe we should bring him in."

"Dilby says no more," Truett intoned. "Too dangerous. You don't know what this guy's goin' to say. And who he's goin' to say it to."

Calpurnia snorted. "Like Dilby wears the britches in this family! We're in charge here. And I say we fire Beaumont."

"Run him over," Emile said.

"Give him to Firebrand," Jim Bob countered.

Luis stepped forward. "I've got a sick magnolia tree that could use him. He'd be a real nice addition to my compost heap."

Maddie held out her hands and shook her head. "No. Don't you see? Maybe his questions play into our hand. We've been so careful with our story, but it begs a few suspicions, even from the sorriest sort of bodyguard—which Beaumont is not."

Truett nodded slowly, the first to see her point. "Maddie's right."

But Calpurnia obviously still had doubts. "So if he's tearin' up the pea patch lookin' for the judge's murderer," she asked, "that's good for us?"

"It's to be expected. We just have to be patient. I'll speak to him. Try to determine his thinking. And if he's *too* suspicious of us, I'll send him packing. I promise."

The group finally nodded their assent, satisfied that Maddie could handle herself with Jack Beaumont. Unfortunately, she wasn't nearly as certain. Maybe Calpurnia's suggestion was worth consideration. Maddie could try to seduce him, distract him until everything worked itself out. He did seem to enjoy those black silk stockings she'd worn to San Francisco.

But she had never put much store in her feminine

assets. Growing up on the streets, she'd been safer to downplay her features. Baggy clothes, slouchy hats—anything she could to make her more inconspicuous to the predators that lurked in the dark alleys and doorways of the Vieux Carré—and the tourists she preyed upon.

Maddie glanced down at the simple summer dress she wore. Though it was pretty, it wasn't the type of outfit to attract a man's attention. "It's not the dress," she murmured, reaching for the library door. "It's what's inside that counts."

By the time she swung the door open, she'd managed to paste a sweet smile on her face. Jack looked up from behind the judge's huge rosewood desk. "I wondered when you'd come in," he said, shuffling some papers before he stood up. "I know you told me you didn't—"

"No," Maddie said brightly, in an attempt at nonchalance. "You have every right to talk to the staff."

"Then you're not angry?"

"Why? Because you're trying to do your job? I trust you, Jack." She sat down in a wing chair and watched him straighten his notes and stuff them into a file folder. "Tell me what you've found."

"They all checked out," he said. "I didn't find anyone with the slightest motive for killing the judge. They all seemed quite loyal—to Lamar and to you."

She wanted to shout out loud, to jump for joy. To scream, "I told you so!" at the top of her lungs. But instead, she maintained her cool and smiled coyly. "I didn't have any doubt."

Gathering her resolve, Maddie slipped her hands beneath her hair and lifted it away from her neck. "There are days I just can't abide this heat. I toss and turn all night until I want to tear every shred of clothing from my body." She winced inwardly, wondering if she'd gone too far. But Jack's attention seemed to be focused on the base of her throat. Taking advantage, Maddie drew her fingers along her collarbone. "I'm positively parched. Would you like to join me on the gallery for some lunch and some cool lemonade?"

Jack licked his lips and glanced up at her. Like a rabbit caught in the middle of the road, Maddie thought with a secret smile. She'd never realized the power of her feminine wiles, but Jack was certainly not immune.

"Lunch would be good," he said.

"Good," Maddie replied, rising as gracefully as she could. She slipped her arm through his and led him toward the door. "I do hope you're well satisfied," she said.

He glanced down at her. "Satisfied?"

"Yes," she purred, her voice not even sounding familiar to her own ears. "About everyone here at Felicity." Maddie slowly stroked his forearm. "Not a one of us has anything to hide."

Somewhere deep within the darkened plantation house, a clock chimed midnight. Jack glanced at his watch to confirm, then pushed himself up from the bed. The house had fallen silent an hour ago. A shudder ran through him as his gaze came to rest on the door to the parlor.

He'd seen a lot of things as a SEAL, done some things that might make a few folks squeamish. But spending time with a dead body gave him the creeps; there was no way around it. At least Truett had pulled guard duty tonight, leaving Jack to catch up on his rack time.

His thoughts wandered to Maddie's bedroom just

beyond the parlor, to the huge four-poster bed she slept in. It was another warm and close night. He wondered if she slept in the silky nightgown she'd worn early that morning in the kitchen, or if the heat had caused her to tear every shred of clothing from her body, as she'd suggested in the library. An image of her naked danced in his head.

She'd be perfect, her skin like silk, her body all soft curves and sweet flesh. She was so small he was certain he could span her waist with his hands; his fingers twitched at the thought. Her hair, her neck, her breasts...he could spend all night exploring the secret pleasures of her body.

Jack flopped back on the bed and threw his arm over his eyes, groaning softly. After all his training, he'd thought he had an ironclad control over himself—over his thoughts, his needs. But when it came to Madeline Parmentier, every ounce of control seemed to evaporate into thin air. Hell, he'd been so distracted he hadn't even been able to objectively analyze his subject. Just who was Madeline Parmentier and what was she up to?

At first he'd pegged her as a social-climbing mercenary, then a chicken-fried Looney Tune. And then, after the crab soup, he'd thought she was just about the most beautiful woman he'd ever met—and a damn good cook to boot. But after their little lunch on the veranda, he wasn't sure what to think. If he didn't know better, he'd have to say she'd turned into Dixie's version of Delilah.

"Women," he muttered, rolling onto his side. He reached over to the bedside table and snatched up his cell phone, then dialed the number for the agency. Knowing Mark, Jack bet he'd have the agency's calls forwarded to his home.

Spenser picked up after only two rings. "S. J. Spade Agency. Beaumont, this had better be you."

"It's me," Jack said.

"How's it going?"

Jack stared up at the intricate plaster medallion on the ceiling above his bed. "Besides the fact that I'm guarding a dead body? Oh, just great. Did you know that's what I was coming here for?"

Spenser chuckled. "A dead body? Samantha's going to love this. Why is it you always get the weird clients?"

"You tell me," Jack muttered. "At least I don't have any trouble keeping track of him. He's not exactly a moving target."

"And why are you guarding this body?"

Jack sighed. "I'll have to get back to you on that. I'm not sure I know myself."

"Well, dead or alive, a body's a body. And Madeline Parmentier is a paying client. Besides, you're an ex-SEAL. If anyone can roll with the punches, you can."

"Well, I'm not planning to roll with anything right now. There's something strange going on here and I want you to help me figure out what it is."

There was a long pause on the other end of the line. "Does this have to do with the job or the woman?"

"Both," Jack said, fumbling for the file folder on the floor beside the bed. "I need you to run background checks for me on an Emile Ferrare, Luis Barrentos, James Robert Preston—also known as Jim Bob—and Calpurnia and Truett Winslow." He carefully spelled out each name and gave Mark a brief physical description. "Check for criminal records in Louisiana, specifically in New Orleans."

"What's going on, Jack?"

"Just humor me. I've got my suspicions, but right now they don't make a lot of sense. There's been a murder, but no one seems to be interested in solving it."

"What about Mrs. Parmentier?"

"Yeah," Jack said, squeezing his eyes shut and rubbing his forehead. "Run a check on her as well—though I don't have a maiden name, so it might be a little tough. Start with her marriage license. She and Lamar were probably married within the last year, most likely in New Orleans."

"I meant, what's going on with you and Madeline Parmentier?"

"Are you asking if I've tried to seduce her?" Jack chuckled. "No, but she's doing her damnedest to seduce me. At least I think that's what she's trying to do."

"You're not sure?"

He pushed himself up in bed and tossed the file on the floor. "I'm not sure about anything right now, Spenser."

"Not every woman is vulnerable to your questionable charms."

"Hey, she's a widow. She's been married to an old man. She's probably...on edge. Can I help it if she's interested?"

"And I suppose you plan to take the edge off?"

"I plan to do my job," Jack said. "That's all you need to worry about. Now, just get me that information. I'll call you back tomorrow night around the same time."

Jack flipped off the cell phone and dropped it on the bed beside him. Then he turned off the bedside light and closed his eyes. But sleep eluded him, and he found his mind filled with possibilities, some so unnerving that he was forced to brush them aside.

"A man is dead," Jack murmured, rubbing his bare chest distractedly, "his body lying in a coffin in the next room. His young and exquisitely beautiful widow, at first glance, seems mournful. Questions are asked, but there are no logical answers. Suspicions are aroused and then...and then the widow suddenly gets friendly." Jack cursed softly. "Be objective, Beaumont. She's hiding something and the closer you get, the more she'll do to distract you. But what is it?"

Did Madeline know who had killed Lamar Parmentier? Was she trying to protect the murderer? Or...or was she trying to protect herself? Jack didn't want to consider that alternative, but he couldn't avoid it. Maddie could have had something to do with her husband's death. Hell, if he looked at it with ice-cold objectivity, he'd know that she could have murdered Lamar Parmentier herself!

As he lay on the bed, his mind whirling with suspicion, a low murmur came from the parlor. He held his breath and listened, trying to make out the voices. There were two, a man and a woman. Calpurnia and Truett? Truett and Madeline?

Slowly, he pushed himself off the bed and crossed the room to stand at the door, where he thought he recognized Maddie's voice. He reached for the knob, but as he turned it, the old metal fittings squeaked, the sound shattering the silence of the house.

He pulled the door open, and in the dim light he saw Maddie standing over the coffin. Jack paused and waited for her to turn around. But she hadn't heard him, or didn't want to acknowledge his presence. Scanning the room, he looked for the man, the mysterious male voice, but she appeared to be entirely alone.

A muffled sob shook her shoulders, and in a few long strides, Jack crossed the room. "Hey," he murmured, placing his hand on her arm. "Hey, it's all right."

Maddie turned her face away, but Jack took her chin and forced her to look at him. Her eyes were moist, but her cheeks were dry. An uneasy suspicion wriggled its way through his mind. What was this? Had weeping become part of her act? Or was she truly upset?

"Don't cry," he murmured. God, he had faced snipers and terrorists and the numbing danger of a nighttime firefight, but toss a few tears in his direction and he wasn't sure what to do.

"I—I can't help it," she said.

He glanced around the room again. "Did someone upset you?"

Maddie wiped away tears that weren't there with a lace-edged handkerchief, then shook her head. "No. I'm fine. I'm sorry."

"Who were you talking to?" The doors to both the veranda and the hallway, as well as to Maddie's bedroom, were closed. Still, someone could be hiding behind the long damask curtains. Or perhaps beneath the small desk near the window. Hell, for all Jack knew, the man Maddie was talking to might even be wedged in the coffin beside old Lamar. "I heard another voice, Maddie."

She blinked, then looked away again, running her palms along the edge of the coffin. She wouldn't meet his gaze. "I—I was talking to Lamar. I find that if I talk to him about the problems of the day, I can sleep better."

"But there was someone else," Jack insisted. Unless she expected him to believe that Lamar talked back. He drew the line at ghosts, especially those that carried on conversations with the living.

Maddie's shoulders stiffened almost imperceptibly. "Someone else?" She glanced around, wide-eyed and innocent. "But there's no one else here."

Jack watched her, now absolutely certain she was lying. Someone *had* been in the room with her. Someone she didn't want Jack to know about. "Where's Truett?"

"He's in the kitchen making a pot of tea. He wanted to give me some time alone."

"I could have sworn I heard…"

Her jaw tensed and she looked at him. Anger, barely hidden, flashed in her green eyes. "I'm alone here. With—with only my memories." Her voice cracked and another sob trembled in her throat. Jack had no choice but to pull her into his arms and comfort her—at least that was what he assumed was expected of him.

But as soon as she pressed her body against his, all suspicions fled from his brain. She felt so good in his arms, a perfect fit. The scent of her hair reached his nose and he pressed his cheek against the silken strands. Her breasts molded to his chest and her hips brushed his from beneath the thin fabric of her gown and robe. He wanted to kiss her. Every instinct he possessed told him to look down into her eyes and cover her mouth with his.

But then he realized that he'd never before held a woman without the intention of bedding her. This wasn't foreplay, this was supposed to be sympathy! A guy just didn't comfort a grieving widow one minute and then toss her on the bed and ravish her the next.

Clenching his teeth, Jack slowly stroked her hair and tried to ignore the flood of heat that pooled in the vicinity of his groin. If he went on much longer, hard evidence of his erotic fantasies would be painfully conspicuous. And pretty embarrassing, especially if he'd read Maddie's motives all wrong.

Maybe she wasn't trying to seduce him. Perhaps he'd just been without a woman for so long that he'd lost the ability to read the signs. Madeline Parmentier was a sad and lonely widow, faced with a future that didn't include the man she loved. Then he felt her palm skim across his naked chest, her fingernails raking through the hair beneath his collarbone. And that particular notion disappeared in an instant.

Reluctantly, Jack grasped her shoulders and gently pushed her away from him. "It's late," he murmured. "Maybe you'd better get some sleep."

She looked up, then nodded. "Maybe that would be best. I—I know it's not part of your job description, but I do appreciate the shoulder to cry on."

He shrugged, then took her hand in his and led her to the door of her bedroom. She gave him one last, long look, enigmatic, mystifying, her secrets still hidden behind her long-lashed eyes. Then she smiled coyly and disappeared into her room.

Leaning back against the door, Jack released a tightly held breath. He rubbed his eyes, then pushed away and slowly began to circle the room. "What was going on in here, Lamar?" he murmured. "Speak up. Tell me what your pretty little wife is up to."

After a thorough search, Jack had no choice but to accept Maddie's words. There *was* no one else in the room. Except, of course, Lamar. Jack studied the coffin for a long moment, then slowly approached. "This insanity must be contagious," he muttered, rapping on the polished wood. "Is anyone in there?"

Jack pressed his ear to the coffin and listened. He didn't expect to hear anything, and to his relief he didn't—but his heart was slamming so hard in his chest he wasn't sure he'd hear even if there was someone breathing inside.

Man, this gave him the willies. With one more burst of courage, he grabbed the lid and tried to pull it up, before he noticed the lock near the ornately carved corner. "All right, we've ruled that out. No one's hiding in the coffin."

One more tour of the room turned up no evidence of another occupant. But then Jack caught sight of something on the rug in front of the bookcase on the far wall. He bent down and picked it up, surprised to find a clump of muddy grass, still wet, the imprint of a shoe heel still evident.

"Well, Mrs. Parmentier, unless you've been strolling in the garden in shoes five sizes bigger than your feet, I'd have to say you've been lying. Someone else has been in this room with you, besides your dear departed Lamar."

Jack slowly turned and stared at the coffin for a long moment. Then he cursed beneath his breath. Why couldn't he leave it alone? Why couldn't he just learn to follow orders without question? He'd been hired to do a job, to guard a body. But every fiber of his being told him there was more to this situation than the obvious, and he couldn't rest until he knew it all.

"Who's the new man in your life, Maddie?" he muttered, rubbing the damp grass between his fingers. "And does he have anything to do with making you a widow?"

The answers were all here at Felicity. He just had to find them.

# 3

MADELINE HEARD the commotion before she saw it. Calpurnia had left the kitchen to answer the front doorbell, and moments later loud voices echoed through the house. Tossing the fresh-picked okra into the sink, Maddie turned and hurried through the dining room and into the foyer. Her gumbo would have to wait.

An older woman stood at the door, dressed entirely in black. But she was decked out in a style more befitting a debutante than a senior citizen. Her dress was all ruffles and bows and geegaws, and she wore a wide-brimmed hat topped with what looked suspiciously like a dead crow.

"I've come to pay my respects to the judge!" the visitor cried, poking at Calpurnia with the tip of her frilly black parasol. "Take me to him immediately."

Calpurnia slapped the offending weapon away. "You get out of my house, Eulalie Rose Peavy! We'll be havin' a proper wake for the judge in time. You can pay your respects then."

Eulalie Rose Peavy? Maddie's heart stopped. She should have known Eulalie would turn up sooner or later. According to Calpurnia, Eulalie had been a regular visitor to Felicity whenever the judge was at home, so much that Calpurnia considered her a pest of the first order. They were old friends, Lamar and Eulalie. In fact, Eulalie had been the best friend of the judge's wife, Miss Sarah, right up until Sarah's sudden death thirty years before. Eulalie had tried to visit every day since the judge's death, but this was the first time she'd managed to get inside the house.

Though she'd never met Eulalie, Maddie should have recognized her immediately from Calpurnia's dead-on description. The times Maddie had visited Felicity as a teenager, she'd kept herself closed in her bedroom when visitors came, afraid that they might suspect who and what she really was. And Eulalie had never made the trip down to New Orleans while Maddie had lived with the judge in his town house.

Like any proper Southern lady, Eulalie Rose never went out calling without a hat. Her hats had become known around Feliciana Parish, and there was no end to the jokes and stories that accompanied the debut of each new creation.

All manner of flora and fauna had perched on the straw brims and crowns, turning Eulalie Rose into a demented version of Carmen Miranda. Calpurnia had gleefully told Maddie that the woman had once worn a rather fetching pillbox topped with yards of pink netting and a dried-up old armadillo's head glued to the back. It had scared half the children into fits of crying at the local Baptist church's Sunday service.

"You can't keep him from me," Eulalie said, her voice taking on a desperate pitch. "We were old friends. I've known the judge longer than you've been around."

"And I know more than you give me credit for, Miz Peavy," Calpurnia replied. "You've been lookin' to land him ever since Miz Sarah left us. You're nothin' but a low-account spinster with the moral character of a harlot."

"Why, I should—"

"Calpurnia?" Maddie stepped forward quickly, certain that Eulalie Rose was about to do Calpurnia grave bodily harm with the business end of her parasol. "Do we have a visitor?"

Eulalie turned to stare at Maddie as she approached. "Is this the little chippy who wormed her way into Lamar's life?"

Maddie winced inwardly. She should have expected that much. To Eulalie—and the rest of the folks around Fells Crossing—she was a stranger, the woman who had managed to drag Judge Lamar Parmentier back to the altar. She held out her hand and gave Eulalie Rose the sweetest smile she could muster. "I'm Madeline Parmentier, Lamar's widow. It's so nice to finally meet you, Miss Peavy. The judge used to talk about you all the time. Won't you come in?"

Calpurnia gasped. "What? You can't—"

"I can and I will," Maddie said, sending the cook a warning glare. "Why don't you make us a nice pitcher of lemonade, Calpurnia? We'll have it on the gallery overlooking the rose garden. Miss Peavy and I are overdue for a chat."

Her display of hospitality had rendered Eulalie speechless, and Maddie was just about to steer the woman to the gallery when the library door swung open and Jack emerged.

"Mr. Beaumont!" Maddie cried, dropping Eulalie's arm and rushing over to him. Ye gods and little fishes, how was she expected to sort this out now? No one in town knew of Jack's arrival except Sheriff Dilby. But once Eulalie found out, it might as well be written in the sky for all to see. She had to think fast!

"I heard shouting," Jack murmured, glancing from Maddie to Calpurnia to Eulalie Rose. "What's going on?"

"That's what I'd like to know," Calpurnia muttered.

"Discretion," Maddie whispered, slipping her arm through his and pulling him forward. "Miss Eulalie Rose Peavy, may I present Mr. Jackson Beaumont of San Francisco. He's a distant relative of Lamar's, come to stay until the funeral." She felt Jack's eyes on her, but she continued to smile benignly, digging her fingers into his arm for emphasis.

"Lamar never told me he had relatives in San Francisco," Eulalie replied in a sulky voice. "We were the best of friends, you know. Ever since he was in short pants and me in crinolines."

"I'm not—"

Maddie pinched Jack's arm to stop him, hoping against hope that he wouldn't give her little white lie away. "What is it, Mr. Beaumont?" she said. "Second cousin thrice removed? Or is it third cousin twice removed? I never can remember."

Jack frowned and cleared his throat, then forced a smile. "I believe it's the second. I mean, the first. Second cousin. Or maybe it was third."

Eulalie Rose watched him with a shrewd eye. "Well, which is it?"

Maddie dropped Jack's arm and grasped Eulalie's, giving it a tug. "Why don't we go on outside while Calpurnia gets us our lemonade?"

But Eulalie stuck tight to her spot, refusing to remove herself from Jack's presence. "You don't look like a Parmentier," she said, examining him shrewdly from beneath the brim of her hat. "How exactly are you related?"

"Ah...by marriage?" Jack replied. "My mother's brother's second wife's cousin, I believe."

Maddie prayed that Eulalie didn't have the brain power to figure out the familial connections. But then,

Southerners had an uncanny knack for understanding even the most distant connections in bloodlines. Especially when it meant they were related to old money or Confederate war heroes.

"And this relative of yours? What was she to Lamar?" Eulalie asked.

Jack glanced at Maddie, obviously for help, but she was still working on his mother's brother. His uncle's second wife had a—

"Well?" Eulalie said.

"What?" Jack countered, dazed and confused.

"Yes, what," Eulalie repeated impatiently. "What was this cousin to Lamar?"

"Are you sure you wouldn't like some lemonade, Miss Eulalie Rose?" Maddie asked in a vain attempt to draw her attention. "We have cookies, too. Very nice cookies. Calpurnia baked them just this morning, didn't you, Calpurnia?"

The cook just snorted, shook her head and folded her arms over her chest. If Maddie wasn't mistaken, Calpurnia was actually enjoying this whole encounter. She'd seen that I-told-you-so look on her face before. Maddie ground her teeth and glared at her. "Go fetch the blasted lemonade and cookies!" she ordered beneath her breath. "And be quick about it!"

Calpurnia gave her a condescending sniff, then pivoted on her heel and headed toward the kitchen. Maddie turned back to Eulalie Rose, ready to make another attempt to distract her attention away from Jack. "I am truly glad you paid us a visit, Miss Eulalie. I—"

"Oh, hush up," Eulalie hissed. "I didn't come here to spend my time talking to you. I came to see Lamar. And if you're not going to take me to him, then I'm just going to have to leave." She gave Jack the once-over, then sneered. "You're no Parmentier that I know. Parmentiers are shorter and skinnier. You're much too...virile. Why, I wouldn't be surprised if you and this little fanfoot here aren't warming each other's bed already." With that, Eulalie slapped her parasol against her palm and stalked to the front door. "Cousins, my backside," she muttered, throwing it open with a flourish before slamming it behind her.

Maddie cursed out loud. "I swear she's the devil's own grandmother! The cold-out meanest woman I ever did meet!" she cried. "How dare she just barge her way into this house and start—"

"What's a fanfoot?" Jack interrupted.

Maddie snapped her head around. "What?"

"A fanfoot. She called you a fanfoot."

She scowled and shrugged. "A hussy. A slut."

Jack's jaw went rigid and his eyes turned cold. "Damn it, she can't talk to you like that! I'll—"

Maddie grabbed him before he got to the door. "Don't," she said. "There's no need to defend my honor. It's nothing more than what the rest of the town thinks. Besides, you'll just get her all riled up again. I'm grateful she's gone."

He gently ran his hands down her arms, then clasped her fingers in his. "Maddie, if my being here is going to hurt your reputation, then—"

"What reputation?" she asked with a laugh. "I have no reputation in Fells Crossing. No one knows me, except for Sheriff Dilby. They just look at me as some gold digger, an across-the-tracks trollop with my eye on Lamar's money. They don't know a thing about me, so they make it all up."

"You should stand up for yourself, starting with Eulalie Peavy."

Maddie sighed. "I don't care what they think of me.

I know who I am. I know that I love Lamar, and that's all that matters."

"Why did you lie to her about me?"

"Because she's the biggest nosybody in the parish. And if she knew you were guarding Lamar's coffin, she'd be callyhooting back to town so fast she'd have bugs on her teeth. And our plan to catch Lamar's murderer would be spoiled. Let them believe what they want," Maddie murmured. "It doesn't bother me."

The truth be told, it did bother her. All Eulalie's nasty comments, and all the whispers Maddie knew were directed her way from town—they were like rubbing salt in an old wound, only to find that it hadn't healed at all. Outside of the kitchen, she had never been confident in her self-worth. She *was* from across the tracks, so far across that in *her* neighborhood she couldn't even hear the train. Had it not been for the judge, she would never have set foot in a house as grand and gracious as Felicity.

"Come on," Jack said, tipping her chin up with his finger. "Jim Bob asked me to help him stack some hay bales. You can walk me down to the stables." With a sweet smile, he took her hand and slipped his fingers between hers.

For a moment she was tempted to pull away, but it felt good to hold on to him, to take comfort in the simple act of kindness he offered. He had jumped to defend her, taking insult in words that were meant to hurt her. If only she'd had someone like him when she was younger, someone to protect her from her mother's vicious tongue and the back of her stepfather's hand.

But now she had Jack, at least for a while yet. And though at times they seemed more like adversaries than allies, she wanted to believe that he had defended her for a reason. Could he care for her, just a little bit? She certainly felt something more than simple friendship toward him, though what it was, she wasn't sure.

They strolled through the rose garden, lingering over the heavily flowered bushes and laughing over the encounter with Eulalie Rose. By the time they reached the stables, Maddie had managed to put Eulalie's nasty words out of her mind. She felt whole again, redeemed by the easy conversation that flowed between herself and Jack, and she didn't want it to end. So she sat down and watched as he and Jim Bob pulled hay bales from the back of Felicity's pickup truck and stacked them in the feed barn.

As she sat, chin in her hand, she studied the stranger who had stepped into her life and taken over her thoughts. He'd tossed his shirt aside and now worked in a pair of black jeans, the chaff and dust rising up around him and clinging to his sweaty chest.

They'd known each other for only a few days, but she sensed he was a good man. He was solid and dependable. An honorable man with an upstanding character. And an honest man. Apprehension snaked through her. How would he feel when he found out she had been lying to him?

*He'll never find out,* Maddie promised herself. Why would he have to? Maybe if they had a future together, learning about her lies would be inevitable. But in time, Jack Beaumont would leave Felicity, leave Louisiana and go home to his job in San Francisco. He'd never have to know where she came from and what she had been.

Maddie turned her face away and pretended to brush a speck of dust from her watery eyes. Nothing could change her past. And even though she'd made something of her life, deep inside she was still that grubby little pickpocket with tangled hair and a smart mouth.

She didn't deserve a man like Jack Beaumont. And she never would.

JACK DIDN'T WANT TO CALL the office. He'd been avoiding it all evening. After spending a pleasant afternoon with Maddie and sharing a long leisurely dinner on the veranda, he didn't want thoughts of her to be tainted by what Mark might tell him.

They'd reached a truce of sorts, a place where they'd both left their suspicions behind. Her edgy moods disappeared and they talked to each other like old friends, laughing and teasing...and deliberately avoiding the subject of her husband's death.

But though their conversation was silly and lighthearted, he couldn't help but notice a sadness in her eyes. He caught it when she looked at him, as if she were staring at a happiness she might never fully possess. Regret, uncertainty, hurt—he detected a bit of each dimming her bright green gaze. And beneath it all, a vulnerability that brought out within him a deep instinct to protect her.

They were attracted to each other, that much was clear. He felt it when he casually touched her hand or basked beneath her pretty smile. But where would that lead? Was her loyalty to her dead husband so strong that she couldn't bring herself to consider another man in her life? And more to the point, did Jack even want to be that man?

With every instinct he possessed, he knew she was hiding something. It stood between them like an impenetrable wall, and as they grew to know each other better, he suspected that it had sparked the sadness in her eyes. Her secrets had to be bad, he thought. So bad that she couldn't risk revealing them.

"So what's the worst they could be?" Jack asked out loud.

He knew the answer to that question and he didn't like it. Even if he was flat-out crazy in lust with Madeline Parmentier, there wasn't any way he could accept what she'd done.

Jack squeezed his eyes shut. Had he found a single shred of proof that she'd been involved in her husband's death? Maybe Madeline Parmentier was exactly as she seemed—a pretty, young, grieving widow who loved her husband dearly. Why did he always imagine the worst? Why couldn't he give her the benefit of the doubt?

After Cynthia, how the hell could he be expected to trust any woman? Jack turned away from the French doors and crossed his bedroom. He snatched up the cell phone from his bedside table and punched in the number for the agency, praying all the time that Mark would have no news for him. Spenser picked up on the third ring and Jack drew in a deep breath.

"It's me. What do you know?" he asked.

He heard Mark shuffle his papers, and waited impatiently. "All right, here it is. I had background checks run on all your names and..."

"And what?"

"And they all have criminal records."

Jack's breath froze in his chest. "What? Say again?"

"Truett and Calpurnia Winslow. Arrested six times between 1963 and 1965. They ran a fortune-telling scam out of a storefront in New Orleans. Emile Ferrare, arrested in 1968 for passing counterfeit bills. He was suspected of running a counterfeit ring, but that couldn't be proved. Luis Barrentos, arrested in 1982 for fencing stolen car radios. And James Robert Preston, in and out of juvie since age nine. Caught running a shell game on Jackson Square two years ago."

"*All* petty criminals?" Jack ran his fingers through his hair and pressed the heel of his hand into his forehead. "That can't be right."

"It is, Beaumont. I double-checked with our contact in New Orleans. Every one of them has a rap sheet."

He didn't want to ask the next logical question, but he couldn't stop himself. "What about Maddie?"

"Maddie?"

"Madeline Parmentier. Did the guy check her record?"

"He couldn't. Couldn't find a marriage license. He went back five years. If they were married, it wasn't in New Orleans. Just on a chance, he checked Vegas, but there was nothing there, either. Without her maiden name, there's no way to check for criminal records. He talked to a few of the judge's colleagues and they were quite surprised to hear that he'd remarried. But then, they all said he was a pretty private guy. He lost his wife thirty years ago, and since then, they say, he hasn't had a woman in his life."

"So this house is filled with suspects?"

"I suppose you could say that. If you believe they had something to do with Lamar Parmentier's death."

"I don't know what I believe," Jack said.

"I could try to get you more, but you're going to have to get her maiden name, maybe find a driver's license or a social security card."

"Yeah, yeah," Jack said distractedly. "I'm just not sure I want to know the truth about her."

"What's going on, Beaumont? I mean, between Madeline Parmentier and you?"

"Nothing," he said.

"You suspect her of being involved in her husband's death. That's not nothing in my book."

"What the hell am I supposed to think? She seems to pull the strings in this house. I'm not sure the others could have planned it without her. They knock off the judge and she collects the inheritance, then splits it with them. I'm sure when the time is right, she'll come up with a properly signed marriage license."

"Well, all I have to say is that you had better be damn sure before you start accusing a client of ours. Samantha is not going to be thrilled about this. In fact, if you want my advice, I'd just leave it alone. Your responsibility is to the client—and the job she hired you for."

"Don't say anything to Samantha," Jack replied. "Just give me some time to figure out what's going on here. I promise, I'll be...discreet."

Mark paused on the other end of the line. "All right. But I want you to call me tomorrow night and give me an update."

Jack sat on the bed and glanced at his watch. "I've got to get to work. I've got the watch tonight. Tomorrow's my day off and I'm going to need a car. Have Charilyn rent one for me and have it dropped at Felicity in the morning. There should be a rental car place in Baton Rouge. If I can't expense it, I'll pay for it myself."

"Where are you going to go?"

"Maybe nowhere. I just don't think I'm going to get to the truth hanging around here. Maybe I'll head down to New Orleans. See the sights, talk to a few of the judge's friends."

"You should try some of the restaurants," Mark said. "Last time we were in New Orleans, we ate dinner at a great place called Delaney's, just off Washington Avenue in the Garden District. They make an amaretto sabayon that's out of this world."

"Yeah, if I can," Jack said, not even sure what a sabayon was. "Although I'm not sure I'll have any time to eat."

"No problem. Hey, I'll talk to you tomorrow, Beaumont."

Jack listened to the click on the other end of the line, then switched off the cell phone and shoved the antenna down with his chin. "Damn, what have I gotten myself into?"

He rolled off the bed, then glanced at his watch. He still had fifteen minutes before he had to relieve Truett in the parlor, fifteen minutes to mull over all he'd learned in the last five. Jack wandered over to the window and looked across the veranda into the garden.

The weather had cooled and thick mist had settled over the live oaks. In the distance, he could see the hazy lights from the stable through the trees. A movement caught his eye, and he watched as a figure hurried from the house into the garden, cast in silver by the light from a gibbous moon. "Maddie," he murmured.

Jack grabbed his shirt from the back of a chair and tugged it on, then slipped out onto the veranda and made his way down to the garden, keeping to the shadows. Carriage lights scattered throughout the landscape illuminated the neat gravel paths, and he followed in the direction that Maddie had fled.

He'd find her and confront her, demand that she tell him exactly what she and her little friends were up to. She'd tell him her name and her background. She'd tell him the truth about her marriage to Lamar Parmentier. And she'd—

Jack froze. The sound of voices drifted through the

mist. He listened, closing his eyes and trying to determine the direction they were coming from. But with the mist, his perceptions were all off. He walked in one direction, and the voices faded. Finally, after a few futile attempts, he got his bearings.

His feet crunched softly on the gravel path as he made his way down toward the riverbank. The mist seemed to thicken the nearer he got to the water until he could barely see in front of his face. But the voices were crystal clear, though disembodied.

Maddie spoke first. "We can't meet in the house anymore," she said. "He heard us last night, in the parlor."

"Does he suspect?" The man's voice was deep and even, but Jack didn't recognize it from among those he knew at Felicity. So Maddie had rushed out of the house to meet a stranger. A boyfriend? A co-conspirator? Or the man who was pulling Maddie's strings at Felicity?

"No. But I think I should tell him. Once he knows, I'm sure he'll understand. We did what we had to do."

"You can't tell him. Not unless it becomes absolutely necessary. Once he knows, we'd be forced to trust him. From what I've heard of this man, he's not the kind to sit back and watch."

Jack leaned forward, squinting, trying to discern their location. But he had to proceed carefully. He didn't know whether he was five feet or fifty feet away, and he didn't want to blunder into their midst. The man didn't sound young, but then Jack could only guess at an age. Maybe forty, maybe older. The night played tricks with a voice. But Jack did recognize a deep Louisiana drawl. And the man sounded well educated.

"We can trust him," Maddie said, "I swear. He won't betray us."

"I'll think about it," the stranger said. He paused for a long moment, and Jack imagined him pulling Maddie into his arms and holding her close, soothing her fears. An unbidden surge of jealousy shot through Jack as he remembered wanting, needing to do the same thing.

"What's wrong, Madeline? You look worried."

She sighed. "Eulalie showed up today. She wanted to pay her respects. She made a real fuss. I think she might cause some trouble in town."

"If you have a hen, she's goin' to cluck," he said with a slow chuckle. "Don't worry. This may look like the back end of bad luck right now, but I've got everything under control. You just do as you have."

Another silence. Jack clenched his jaw, fighting back another wave of anger and jealousy that threatened to suffocate him. With a silent curse, he stepped back, the gravel shifting beneath his foot. The sound amplified in the damp air and Jack held his breath.

"What was that?" Maddie said. He could imagine her staring into the darkness, could feel her looking in his direction. He took a step forward. It was time to find out the truth about Madeline Parmentier.

MADDIE'S HEART SKIPPED. Someone was out there, hiding in the mist, waiting, watching them both. Had Truett come looking for her? Or was it simply a night animal? She turned back to her companion. "You have to go," she whispered. "It's not safe."

He nodded, then stepped back, searching the surrounding shadows as she had. "Take care, Madeline. This will all be over soon. I promise."

Maddie reached out and squeezed his hand. "No, you take care."

He hurried off into the darkness, the mist swallowing him up. A long minute passed. Maddie sighed, closing her eyes and saying a silent prayer. There was no one out there, no one to—

"Hello, Maddie."

With a soft gasp, she spun around. A tall figure stood just ten feet away, his features shimmering in the mist and the moonlight. She swallowed hard, her heart slamming in her chest. "Jack! What are you doing here?"

He took a step closer. "I could ask you the same question. But would you give me the right answer?"

"I was just taking a—a walk," she replied. Maddie glanced around. "It's such a…" She winced inwardly, about to say "hot." Instead, she forced a smile. "It's an odd night. Don't you think?"

"Very odd."

Maddie slowly approached him until she could make out his face. "So, what are you doing out here?" she asked lightly. "If I didn't know better, I'd think you were following me."

"Do you need to be followed?" Jack asked.

Maddie laughed, the sound strained even to her own ears. Why was he acting so obtuse? "What is that supposed to mean? I was simply taking a walk. Am I supposed to ask your permission every time I leave the house?"

"Maybe so," Jack replied. "I do worry about you."

A secret thrill shot through her at his words. But then it dissolved as her gaze took in the hard set of his mouth, his icy eyes. In that instant, she knew he'd heard. Maybe not all of it, but enough to know that she'd been out here with a man. "You—you don't have to. I can take care of myself."

The corners of his mouth curled slightly, cynically, and he took another step toward her. "If I don't protect you, who will?"

She bristled, certain he was baiting her, challenging her. "I told you when you came here that I didn't need your protection."

"Maybe not from your husband's murderer. Do you know who killed Lamar?"

Maddie felt as if he'd punched her in the stomach. Her eyes watered and she gasped for breath. "No! Why would you ask a question like that?"

He shrugged. "I don't know. Maybe I'm curious?"

"I—I swear to God, I had nothing to do with Lamar's murder."

He took one more step. "Tell me the truth, Maddie. I'll find out sooner or later."

"I am telling you the truth."

One last step and he was standing so close she could feel the heat radiating from his body. His shirt was unbuttoned and she fought the crazy urge to reach out and run her fingers along the light dusting of hair, to trace a path from his collarbone to his hard belly. Anything to distract him from such a disturbing line of questioning.

In the end, she clenched her fists at her sides and dragged her attention back to his face, to the hard planes and angles that she found so incredibly attractive. But she couldn't hold his gaze for long, the intensity of it burning into her brain until she was certain he could read her thoughts.

"Look at me, Maddie."

She shook her head and kept her gaze averted. But

he tipped her chin up, holding firm until she was forced to meet his eyes.

"Look at me and tell me again. Tell me the truth."

Anger and indignation slowly pulsed through her. What right did he—a perfect stranger—have to question her feelings for Lamar? Did he think because they were mildly attracted to each other he could demand to know her every secret? "You want the truth?" she snapped.

"That's all I've ever wanted."

She stared into his eyes, her gaze unwavering. "Then here's the truth," she said in a calm, even voice. "Lamar means more to me than any man I'll ever know. I'll love him forever. And I could never *ever* do anything that would hurt him." She paused, trying to calm her temper.

For a long time, Jack didn't say anything. She expected anger, more accusations. But as she stared up at him, the mistrust slowly dissolved from his eyes. Relief washed over her. He believed her! "Are you satisfied?" she finally asked.

"There's only one thing that will satisfy me," he murmured, his gaze skimming over her face to rest on her lips.

"And what is that? Please tell me. I'd be happy to oblige."

"This," Jack murmured. He grabbed her arms, his hands hot on her bare flesh, and pulled her against him. She drew in a sharp gasp, but the sound of the blood rushing to her head, the pulse pounding in her temples, obliterated everything else.

He lowered his head until his mouth was nearly on hers. "God help you if you're lying to me, Maddie." He moaned softly. "And God help me."

With that, he brought his mouth down over hers. It

was hot, urgent, drawing her into a kiss that erased all thoughts of Lamar from her head. She wanted to resist, needed to push Jack away. His kiss had come out of nowhere, blindsiding her with its intensity. But she didn't want to fight him and she opened beneath him, unable to deny him such intimacy. The taste of him was like a drug and before long she'd lost all capacity to draw away. She needed more...longer, deeper, warmer.

Maddie had never been kissed like this before. Nothing in her experience had prepared her for the absolute power he held over her. She wanted to pull away, for she knew that conceding to him now would be something she'd regret later. He'd demanded the truth and she'd told him only part of it. There were so many more things she was hiding, so much that she might never reveal.

But she could reveal one thing—to herself, at least. She loved the way Jack Beaumont kissed. And after he stopped, if he ever stopped, she would dream about his mouth on hers, crave it like an addiction, need it as much as she needed air to breathe.

His lips shifted above hers, his tongue probing deeply, teasingly, drawing her in. She couldn't stop him. She didn't want to stop him. Maddie pressed her palms into his hard chest, but she couldn't bear to push him away. Instead, she slowly raked her nails over his hot skin.

Jack groaned, the sound coming from deep in his throat. In that instant, she realized that she wasn't as powerless as she'd thought. He wanted her as much as she wanted him. She slid her hands up to his shoulders, then around his neck to furrow through the hair at his nape.

*More*, her mind screamed. *I want more.*

She tugged on his hair, pulling his mouth from hers. Through a haze, her gaze traveled over his handsome features, a visual caress. Maddie felt an overwhelming need to assure herself that he was real and not just some errant fantasy.

Licking her lips, she leaned forward and pressed her mouth to his bare chest. She brushed aside his shirt, hands trembling, her breath coming in short gasps, her heart pounding. She tasted his skin, damp from the mist that shrouded them from the real world.

Jack nuzzled his face in her hair and sighed softly. "Why did you come down here to the river, Maddie?"

"To take a walk," she replied.

"Did you know I'd follow you? Did you want me to follow you?"

She nodded, looking up at him. Desire burned brightly in his eyes, a heat so intense it sent a flood of warmth racing through her veins. "Yes," she murmured. "I mean, no. I didn't want you to follow me. But I wanted this."

He kissed her again, sweeping her into that dream world that existed only when their mouths touched. For the first time in her life, she felt wanted, as if the woman she was made a difference somehow. Jack was kissing *her*, he was touching *her*.

"Who was he, Maddie?" Jack murmured against her lips. "Who did you come down here to meet?"

"You," she whispered, her mind crazy with need. "I came here for you." She pulled him back into the kiss, but his mouth grew still beneath hers. Confused by his mercurial moods, she looked up at him.

His eyebrow arched and a tiny smile played at the corners of his mouth. "Liar," he said.

The word cut her like a dagger, all the warm desire seeping out of the wound until she nearly shivered beneath his icy gaze. "Is that what this is all about?" she cried. "Do you think that if you muddle my head with passion, I'll tell you something you want to know?"

"Who was he, Maddie?"

She yanked her arms out of his grasp. "He is none of your damn business, that's who he is."

"As long as you're my business, then he is, too."

"Well, then, maybe you should leave. Maybe you should go back to San Francisco. We don't need you here. *I* don't need you." Though the words came out full of raw anger, she didn't mean any of it. She didn't want him to leave Felicity, but what choice did she have? She couldn't tell him the truth, and he didn't believe her lies.

Jack cursed softly. "Dammit, Maddie, why can't you just be honest with me? If you have some guy on the side, tell me."

She stiffened her spine and faced him with a frigid calm. "There is no one else. And I had nothing to do with Lamar's death. That's all I'm going to say. If you don't believe me, then leave. I'll give you your return ticket. Just go. Get out of here."

His expression softened and she could read regret in his eyes. But when he moved to touch her again, she stepped back, beyond his reach. "I'm sorry," he said, reaching out again.

But this time she held out her hand to stop him. "Don't!"

"What are you afraid of, Maddie? What happened between us was nothing you or I can control."

"We have to," she said. "Because I never want it to happen again."

"You're not married anymore. What's to stop us?"

He was right. She couldn't control herself around him. And there was nothing to stop them, nothing standing between them but a pack of lies that seemed to grow larger every day.

"Just go," she pleaded. "Leave me alone."

"Maddie, I—"

"Go!" she shouted, her voice echoing over the misty river. "I don't want you here."

He studied her for a long minute, and she found it nearly impossible to maintain her composure. Tears pressed at the corners of her eyes—tears of frustration, anger and then the inevitable sadness. She didn't need him. She didn't need anyone!

Maddie Delaney had lived her life by her own rules. She had controlled her destiny; she had made all the decisions. And now this man had stepped into her life and shaken the very core of her being. When Jack kissed her, she forgot who she was...what she'd been.

"Please," she murmured. "How many times do I have to ask you? Go. I need to be alone."

He swore softly, then turned and disappeared into the mist. Maddie listened as his footsteps crunched along the gravel path. When she could no longer hear him, she brought her hands to her face and covered her eyes.

"Madeline?"

She spun around, the warm voice like a balm to her nerves. He must have been waiting until Jack left, waiting to comfort her. With a soft sob, she ran toward him and threw herself into his arms. "Did you hear? He kissed me. And then he called me a liar. Oh, Lamar, what am I going to do?"

Lamar Parmentier gently patted her back. "Tell him the truth, Madeline. Tell him that I'm still alive. And after that, tell him we aren't married. That we've never been married."

# 4

THERE WAS ONE WAY to find out what he really needed to know. Jack decided to spend some time talking to the folks who lived in Fells Crossing. If Eulalie Rose Peavy was any indication, there would be plenty of opinions on the Widow Parmentier, her late, lamented husband, and what had really happened at Felicity the night the judge died.

Jack's mind flashed back to the previous night, to all that had happened on the riverbank. It seemed like a dream, evaporating like morning dew under the rising sun. He had kissed her, that much he did remember. And the memory of her mouth beneath his was enough to bring all the desire flooding back again.

But why had it happened? He'd convinced himself that he shouldn't want her, at least not until he knew every secret she kept. But there was something growing between them that he could no longer deny, a spark that had burst into flame the moment his lips touched hers.

Beneath that vulnerable exterior, he'd discovered an unexpected strength, a devotion to her dead husband that he coveted for himself. What would it feel like to claim Maddie as his own, to have her love him the way she professed to love Lamar? Hell, he was jealous of a dead man!

Jack cursed out loud. And then there was the man she'd gone to meet. The thought of him turned Jack's desire to doubt in the blink of an eye, and he remembered the anger between them last night. Who the hell was this guy?

Jack wanted to believe in Maddie, but every instinct told him that he shouldn't. And when it came to women, he had learned to listen to his instincts. Cynthia had left him with that. And though every bone in his body told him that the truth would destroy what he and Maddie had begun to build, he still had to know.

Jack opened the front door and stepped outside. Exhaustion dogged his every movement. After guarding Lamar all night long, he'd tried to get some sleep. But images of Maddie had plagued his mind. Maybe he ought to have accepted her suggestion to leave. He certainly wasn't making his life any easier by staying at Felicity.

After tumbling out of bed, he had gone looking for Maddie in the kitchen, but she hadn't been there. Calpurnia had given him some half-mumbled excuse, saying her mistress was out riding with Jim Bob and wouldn't return until after lunch, but Jack suspected that Maddie was simply trying to avoid him.

Why had he pushed her so? Why couldn't he just accept her explanations and leave her alone? He saw the truth in her eyes, or what he believed was the truth, and yet he couldn't allow himself to buy her story—or her resistance.

Jack strode down the front steps, then noticed the sporty red convertible parked in the drive. Emile, dressed in his chauffeur's uniform, was polishing the hood with a rag. "Your car's here," he called, squinting through his spectacles. "I'd be happy to drive you into town. Been years since I drove me one these ragtops."

Jack didn't have the heart to refuse the old man. "Nah," he said. "I think I'm going to walk." Besides not trusting Emile behind the wheel, Jack needed physical exercise. In the navy, he'd done a lot more than just sit beside a coffin and lie around in bed until noon. The food here had already added a few unneeded pounds.

He got vague directions from Emile, then set off at a fast pace to Fells Crossing. The walk wasn't nearly as long as Jack expected, and it was rather pleasant, all things considered. Birds crowded the arching limbs of the live oaks that lined the narrow road to town. Dogs barked and little children shouted from wide lawns, creating a noisy counterpoint to the chattering of a mockingbird. An armadillo skittered across the road and disappeared into the dense undergrowth. And always, the scent of flowers, a heady perfume, followed him wherever he went.

Jack drew a deep breath. He was really beginning to like the South—the smell of green in the air, the easy languor that hung over everything and everyone. There was time to breathe here, time to think. And time to appreciate the simple things—like the beauty of Maddie Parmentier's green eyes, the sweet curves of her body, the tranquilizing sound of her voice.

Fells Crossing was a tidy little town, made up of redbrick buildings and white clapboard houses, some dating back nearly two centuries. The sign on the outskirts of town boasted 1500 stalwart citizens. "One of them will tell me what I need to know," Jack murmured as he headed toward the downtown area.

He found the sheriff's office on the right. A dopey-looking deputy paused from polishing the bars of the town's only jail cell to inform Jack that Sheriff Dilby was down at Finis Capshaw's place, getting his weekly haircut.

The barbershop was only a block farther. Jack looked through the plate glass window to find the tiny shop nearly full. Every one of the four available waiting chairs was taken, as well as the one in front of the mirror. A hulk of a man, white haired and florid faced and dressed in a crisply pressed uniform, patiently sat as Finis snipped away. Jack pulled the screen door open and a bell tinkled above his head.

The customers swiveled to watch his entrance. He smiled wanly at their curious expressions. They obviously didn't cotton to strangers invading their domain. Unless he played his cards very carefully, he wouldn't get much out of this group.

"Sheriff Dilby?" Jack said, approaching the man in the chair.

"I was the last time I signed my name, son. What can I do for you?"

The group gave that little joke a hearty guffaw and Jack smiled. "I'm Jack Beaumont. I'm a distant relative of Lamar Parmentier. Third cousin, twice removed. I'm staying up at Felicity until the funeral." Dilby knew the real reason for his visit to Felicity—that he was guarding Lamar's body—but Jack wasn't sure who else was privy to that information. According to Maddie, this whole thing was Dilby's grand plan to catch a killer, and Jack didn't put much store in the sheriff's abilities.

Sheriff Dilby studied him for a long moment, then nodded. "So you are."

Jack leaned nearer to the sheriff and lowered his voice. "If you have a moment, I was hoping we could talk. About Lamar's...death? Maybe after your haircut?"

The sheriff pushed Finis's hand away, then yanked the towel from around his neck as he pushed out of the chair. "I'm afraid I've got to get back to work, son. Maybe some other time." With that, Dilby pressed a five-dollar bill into the barber's hand and brushed past Jack. He grabbed his hat from the rack and was out the door before Jack could manage another word. For a large man, he moved like a jackrabbit.

"Been a little edgy lately, that one," Finis explained with a sigh. "Ever since Lamar's passin'. Some folks in town are thinkin' we ought to call in the Federal Bureau of Investigation." Finis came around in front of Jack and looked up at him with a narrow-eyed gaze, his eyes magnified by the thick, horn-rimmed glasses he wore. "You lookin' for a trim, son?"

Jack shook his head, glancing around the group. "No. I'm fine. Why do you think he won't call in the FBI?"

Finis slowly circled around to the other side as he examined Jack's hair, plucking at it with his fingers. "You was in the military, wasn't you."

Jack blinked in surprise. "Yeah. Navy. But I've been out for over a year."

"I know hair. I could give you a real nice cut for a good price. Slick as one of them navy barbers."

Jack shook his head. "About Sheriff Dilby...and the FBI."

"Hmm. He's a powerful proud man, he is."

"High-minded and contrary's more like it," a tall, rangy man muttered from one of the vinyl chairs near the window.

"Now then, Dewey Dilby, is that any way to talk about your very own twin brother? Just because Dudley fired you as his deputy doesn't give you leave to be bad-mouthing the man."

"You're Sheriff Dilby's brother?" Jack asked.

The man nodded, tipping his tattered straw hat, then replacing it low over his eyes. To Jack's delight, Finis proceeded to introduce the rest of the crowd. Besides Dewey, there was Roscoe Saunders, the town's used-car dealer, and Waymore Riley, the postmaster. Custis Polk, the town's banker, and Emmett Duvelle, the owner of the general store, rounded out the group.

"So yer stayin' with the Widder Parmentier," Roscoe said.

"Are you sure you wouldn't be wantin' me to give you a trim?" Finis asked. "Yer lookin' a mite shaggy."

"Really, Mr. Capshaw. I'm perfectly happy with my hair. What do you all know about Lamar's death?"

"You mean his murder?" Dewey asked.

Custis snorted. "Was it murder? Some folks 'round here think that's all a pack of lies. The old guy died in his sleep, that's what I heard."

Waymore shook his head. "I heard tell that Yancey Hamilton saw the judge just the other night, driving around in that big ole black car of his."

"Spirits," Finis said, reaching out for Jack's hair with his comb. "I could do you up real fine. Jes' like them big-city barbers. Stylin'. Jes' some fancy way to say haircut. I know stylin'. I got me a can of mousse right over there."

"What do you mean by spirits?" Jack said.

Finis gently pushed Jack toward the chair. "Ghosts. Phantasms. Specters. Could be that Lamar is hauntin' the corporeal world."

"Why would he do that?"

The barber wrapped a towel around Jack's neck. "Maybe he don't want anyone hornin' in on his territory. Romancin' that pretty wife of his."

"Or mebbe he jes' wants to hang about till the funeral," Dewey hypothesized. "Check out what ever'one says about him. Spook the ones that ain't nice."

Jack winced as he heard the scissors snip close to his ear. But he wasn't about to interrupt the conversation with any vain concerns about his hair. Hell, Finis could shave his head if it meant Jack could learn more about Maddie and her late husband. "So you all believe in ghosts?"

"Yep."

"Sure."

"Never a doubt in my mind."

They all answered in the affirmative. There was no arguing the point, but Jack refused to concede that he'd heard the voice of a ghost last night at the river. Maddie had been talking to a man, a flesh and blood man. Though Jack hadn't actually seen him, that certainly didn't mean he was a ghost. "Mrs. Parmentier doesn't talk too much about her husband's death," Jack finally said.

Dewey shrugged. "That's prob'ly 'cause she weren't here when Lamar died. She come to town the very next day. They had to call her down in New Orleans."

"Are you sure?"

The entire group nodded. "Yep," Roscoe said. "And she caused a big stir when she arrived. None of the folks in town knew the judge had cut the cake. He was always a private-type man. But a man his age, married to a looker like her... Well, I'd be shoutin' it from the church steeple, if it was me."

"You know, they're sayin' she bewitched him," Emmett commented. "He was pure in love with his first wife, Sarah. Swore he'd never marry another. Dead or alive, he would love her till the last pea was out of the dish. And then this one shows up."

Dewey sighed and shook his head. "Even for an important man like the judge, life does get daily," he said. "Mebbe he jest got horny."

"A man his age ain't interested in that sort of thing!" Finis countered.

Custis laughed. "Don't you be tellin' my wife that!"

"Heck, look at old Minyard Barrow. He fathered a baby when he was eighty-one years old!"

"I still got myself a few needs," Waymore said.

"Just 'cause the flag don't go all the way up the pole don't mean you can't salute," Roscoe said.

The conversation quickly deteriorated into a rousing panel discussion on the sex lives of the over-sixty set, with everyone but Finis standing up on the side of the septuagenarian sex drive. By the time Finis yanked the towel from Jack's neck, they had moved on to female erogenous zones, a subject more suited to the beauty parlor than the local barbershop.

To Jack's surprise, he got a good haircut at a good price, just as Finis had promised. He tipped the barber generously, said goodbye to his newfound friends and quickly stepped outside, not willing to get caught up in the debate over battery-powered sexual aids.

But the screen door had barely slammed behind him before he felt a poke in his side. He turned around to find Eulalie Rose Peavy, her parasol drawn. Today she'd eschewed the black mourning for green-and-yellow polka dots, in a fabric that looked strangely like his mother's shower curtains. On Eulalie's hat perched two dead canaries, lost in a bunch of plastic lemons.

"I heard you talkin' in there," she said, her tone accusatory. "If you want to know the truth about Lamar's death, you should have come to me!"

Jack opened his mouth, then snapped it shut. What would Eulalie know about that night at Felicity that the rest of the town didn't? "Miss Peavy, I—"

"She killed him! She did!"

He didn't know what to say. The vicious look in Eulalie's eyes startled him, for he hadn't imagined her as anything more than a slightly eccentric spinster. He saw deep hate in her expression. "Maddie?"

"Is that what you call her? I prefer Jezebel."

"And how did Maddie kill him?" he asked.

Eulalie leaned forward, and Jack nearly passed out from the profusion of perfume that wafted up around him. Lemons. It must be the theme for the day. She had surely doused herself with it before she left the house. "Conjugal calisthenics," Eulalie explained, sending him a knowing look.

"What?"

"She killed him in bed, you half-wit. Isn't it obvious? She's a sex-starved alley bat. She used her cunnin' wiles to lure him into the marital bed and then she killed him. As sure as God made little chickens."

"Miss Peavy, I don't think—"

The woman jabbed her parasol into his chest. "You listen to me, young man. You watch yourself around her. She could do the same to you! You'll be pushin' up daisies just 'cause you let her scratch your itch." With that, Eulalie popped open the parasol, turned neatly on her heel and flounced off.

Baffled by her bizarre revelations, Jack could only stare after her. Of all the theories about Lamar Parmentier's death, Eulalie's was surely the most original. He'd heard of older men who'd died in flagrante delicto. But he doubted that...

Jack blinked hard. Geez, could Eulalie's explanation possibly be true? Was that what everyone at Felicity was hiding? Maybe Maddie *did* have something to do with her husband's death, something so embarrassing that she couldn't bear the thought of public exposure.

His mind raced back to the night before, to the man Maddie had met on the riverbank. A slow replay of the conversation didn't yield any new clues. Unless...Maddie had been speaking to Sheriff Dilby. Maybe that's who she'd met in the dark last night. The sheriff would have to be in on it, he'd have to know the truth. What if *he* were protecting Maddie, as well?

Had they fabricated a murder to cover an accidental death? Jack raked his hands through his hair. "Well, this is a strange turn of events." Somehow, when he'd imagined learning of Madeline Parmentier's complicity in her husband's death, he'd expected to feel a flood of self-righteous anger.

Instead, all he really felt was an overwhelming curiosity. And a strong desire to find out firsthand what a woman like Maddie actually *did* in the bedroom to send a man over the edge—and into the grave.

MADDIE SAW JACK the instant she stepped out of the post office. She still wore her riding clothes buff-colored breeches, spit-shined boots and a loose cambric shirt that clung to her damp skin. Her hair was pulled up on top of her head and flyaway tendrils clung to her temples and neck.

She'd left Jim Bob back at the stables and had ridden Tansy into town to cool her down after their morning ride. The filly stood patiently waiting, her reins twisted through the railing near the front door of the post office.

Maddie adored riding. The judge had first brought

her to Felicity three months after he'd taken her in, and she'd fallen in love with every horse in his stable. Perhaps it had been her long-denied adolescence that finally asserted itself. Horses had been a convenient substitute for the other obsession of teenage girls—teenage boys. She had begged the judge to allow her to ride and he couldn't refuse, giving her her first lesson that very day.

Riding through the silent fields surrounding Felicity had brought Maddie a freedom from her past. Her horse didn't care who she was or what she'd done, and there was no one to hide from in the great outdoors. She'd become a good rider, taking advantage of her sporadic weekends in the country, rewards for doing well in her New Orleans school.

But she could never bring herself to ride into town or to visit the various neighbors along the river road, no matter how hard the judge pressed her. Perhaps she was frightened of the questions she might have to answer. Who was she? Where did she come from? And what was she doing at Felicity?

She was Maddie Delaney, pickpocket extraordinaire. She'd come from the streets of New Orleans, yanked out of the gutter by a kindly man. And she was having the first truly wonderful time of her life. So she had kept to herself, confident in her solitude—and greedy to preserve her happiness.

It had taken all her courage to ride into town today. She still feared the questions, but now she had answers. She was Madeline Parmentier, the widow of Judge Lamar Parmentier. She came from New Orleans via Paris. And she had every right to be at Felicity. At least, that was the story she planned to tell.

She had all the answers down pat. But what about Jack? She'd half expected him to leave as she had demanded, taking *his* questions with him. The last place she expected to see him was Fells Crossing. For a long moment, all manner of fears raced through her head, every problem that could result from a wrong word here, a stupid assumption there.

She stared across the street and noticed that he stood in front of the barbershop. Even from this distance she could see that his hair was a bit shorter. A wave of relief washed over her. He'd simply come for a haircut. That was all.

"I'd better make sure that's all," Maddie murmured to herself. She hurried down the post office steps and grabbed Tansy's reins, tugging the horse into step behind her. "Hello," she called, giving Jack a hesitant wave.

He turned to look at her, then shaded his eyes against the bright midday sun. "Maddie?"

Her hands fluttered to her hair and she tucked a stray strand behind her ear as her mind flashed back to the kiss they had shared the night before. Just the thought of him holding her, tasting her, brought a flush to her cheeks.

The kiss had been completely inappropriate. After all, she was a widow, still in love with her husband— or that's what he was supposed to think. And he was an employee. But all that seemed to fall away when they were together. Their attraction had been too strong to resist.

But as she watched him cross the street, she realized that she was feeling more than just simple lust. The kiss had only confirmed what she'd tried so hard to deny. With his gentle charm and his stubborn insistence on the truth, he'd found a spot in a secret corner of her heart. She should hate him, but she couldn't. Instead, she thought about him every waking minute and dreamed about him when she slept.

He wanted her and she'd never been wanted, not once in her entire life, and certainly not by a man as strong and good as Jack Beaumont. Deep inside, she wanted to believe that he would be able to handle the truth about her past and care about her anyway. But could she take that risk? Could she believe that there was something more between them than just lust?

"What are you doing here?" Jack asked. "And who's your friend?"

She glanced back at her horse. "This is Tansy. I was just out riding and I—well, I needed to stop at the post office and Tansy needed to cool down. A friend in New Orleans promised to send me a new cookbook and I was hoping it had come."

"Another friend?"

"I do have friends," Maddie said. "Even a few who aren't horses." The truth be told, she had acquaintances, associates, people who knew her from the restaurant. The cookbook was coming from her manager at Delaney's, Anne Ladret, whom she considered a girlfriend. But her only true friend, a friend she could trust with all her secrets, was Lamar. And the only family she could claim was the group who worked at Felicity. "I'm heading home. Did you drive or walk?"

"Walked," Jack said. "I'll go back with you, if that's all right."

Maddie smiled and nodded. They strolled down the middle of the dusty main street, silence standing between them. She knew she should bring up what had happened the night before, but she didn't want to argue with him. And she didn't want to spoil the memory.

As they walked, Maddie could feel the eyes of the

townsfolk on her. They were speculating again, about the Widow Parmentier and the handsome man she'd invited to stay at Felicity. She smiled and nodded at everyone who passed, but she got only stoney expressions and whispered comments in return.

"You don't have many friends here in Fells Crossing," Jack observed.

Maddie's face grew warm with embarrassment. "I suppose that's true. They all think they know who I am. But they don't."

"Why don't you tell them?"

Maddie shrugged. The folks in Fells Crossing were the least of her worries. "What good would it do? They'll always believe what they want to believe."

"They believe you killed your husband."

Maddie's heart lurched in her chest and she stopped. "What? They—they think *I* killed Lamar?" Tears sprang to the corners of her eyes, not out of humiliation but frustration. She shouldn't be surprised. After all, Jack had said as much last night, right before he kissed her. This lie would ruin her before much longer. "I told you, I could never, ever hurt Lamar."

Jack reached out and touched her cheek. "I'm sorry, I didn't mean to upset you." He paused, studying her intently. "And I'm sorry about last night. I shouldn't have pressed you. You have a right to your privacy. I was completely out of line." He smiled. "Forgive me?"

"For the questions?" Maddie asked. She swallowed hard. "Or—or for the kiss?"

"Both," he murmured with a contrite smile.

Maddie nodded, disappointed that he wanted to apologize for something she'd thoroughly enjoyed. But there was a certain chivalry to the gesture. And the tension between them had subsided. "I suppose I can't be angry at you. I need one champion here in Fells Crossing."

"You know, it's actually pretty funny what they think...or what Eulalie thinks."

"I'm not sure I want to know," Maddie said with a wince.

"She thinks you killed Lamar in bed."

A giggle bubbled up from Maddie's throat. She tried to keep from laughing, but couldn't. The notion was so utterly ridiculous! First, that Maddie even possessed the talent for such a feat. And then, that she would apply those talents to a man she thought of as a surrogate father, a man twice her age.

"She said you had an insatiable appetite for conjugal calisthenics. I must say, I was rather intrigued. I knew you had more than one talent. There's cooking. And riding. And now..."

She sent him a skeptical glance. "Well, that's one rumor I can unequivocally deny. Lamar did not die in my bed."

"Maybe you should take out a newspaper ad," Jack suggested.

"What?"

"To clear up the misconceptions around town. I'd be perfectly willing to testify that you don't possess any extraordinary powers. That is, if I had firsthand knowledge," he said. "I've always dreamed of meeting a woman who could render a man unconscious in bed."

All the anger and accusation that hung between them from the night before was gone, forgotten, replaced by teasing banter and sly innuendo. They were friends again. "All it really takes is a large hammer and a well-aimed blow," Maddie said. "I'll show you sometime."

They held hands as they walked, the warm day slowly repairing the rift between them. When they were finally past the outskirts of Fells Crossing, Jack slipped his arm around her waist.

"Tell me about you and Lamar," he said, staring off into the thick woods that edged the road. "Tell me about the night that he died."

"There's not much to tell," Maddie said, weary of the questions, but reluctant to start another argument between them. At least she could explain that night without a litany of lies. "I wasn't here. I—I was in New Orleans, at his—*our* town house. When I got here the next morning, he was—gone."

"What were you doing in New Orleans?"

"I—I don't remember. Shopping, I think. Calpurnia called me and told me that I had to come to Felicity right away. Truett came down and picked me up."

"Did you love him, Maddie?"

She looked at Jack, meeting his gaze directly. "I still do," she said, glad that she didn't have to lie about that. She loved Lamar like she might have loved her father, if she'd known her father. But the man who had given her life hadn't wanted her, hadn't even stuck around until her first birthday. "The day we met, it changed my life."

"There was a big difference in your ages. Didn't that bother you?"

"We became friends. I trusted him and he believed in me. I didn't have much when I was younger. My family wrote the book on dysfunction. Lamar was...steady. Patient and kind." She took a long breath. "Come on, I'll show you a shortcut to Felicity."

She gave Tansy's reins another tug and led the horse to the edge of the road. A trampled path, one she knew quite well, appeared in the thick undergrowth. "Go ahead," she told Jack. "Just follow the path."

She knew what lay ahead, but it always seemed to take her by surprise, anyway. The crumbling walls, the gothic arches above the broken windows. The crepe myrtles on either side of the entrance.

The tiny chapel had stood in this spot since before the Civil War. Lamar had told her the story of how it had burned the night the Yankees arrived on Felicity. The mistress of Felicity, Eliza Fells Parmentier, couldn't bear to rebuild. So she had left it as it was, a testament to all that her family had lost during the war.

Jack stopped on the path when he saw the ruins, the old brick walls still visible through the tangle of kudzu. "What is this?" he asked.

Maddie dropped Tansy's reins and stepped up beside him. "The Fells family chapel. Augustus Fells built it for his only child, Eliza. She was married in this very spot to John Bowden Parmentier. He died in the War Between the States, but not before Eliza gave birth to Lamar's great-grandfather."

"It's beautiful," Jack said, staring at the myriad colors of the broken, stained-glass windows, the afternoon light casting a rainbow on the forest floor.

"I like to come here." Maddie picked her way among the thick vines and stood near the old crepe myrtles. A breeze ruffled the trees and the tiny white flowers showered over her. "It's like snow," she said, laughing, tipping her face up.

She turned and stepped inside the chapel. Jack followed her, coming to a stop behind her, so close she could feel the heat from his body. They stood silently, staring at the stone altar.

"It didn't sound like a grand passion," Jack said.

Maddie glanced over her shoulder. "What didn't?"

"Your marriage to Lamar."

She turned back to the altar. "It wasn't," she said bluntly. "But then, I never really believed in that kind of love—the fireworks and angel choirs kind."

"And now?"

Her breath caught in her throat. "I'm not sure what I believe anymore. I do know that there are times when I wish Lamar were standing right here. I could talk to him about anything. He always knew the right thing to do."

"Talk to me," Jack said.

"I—I don't have anything to say."

He leaned over her shoulder, his voice soft against her ear. "Tell me how you feel, Maddie. When I kiss you." He ran his knuckles along her neck. "When I touch you. Do you think about Lamar? Or do you see the same fireworks I see? Tell the truth, Maddie—you're in a church."

She shook her head. "No." The single word came out like a strangled plea. She drew a deep breath as she pulled away and faced him. "I don't think of Lamar. Lamar never made me feel...that way."

A rueful smile twitched her lips. She had to tell him now, all of it. That Lamar was still alive, that she had never been married to him. That everything Jack knew about her was a lie. "I don't make a very convincing widow, do I?" she murmured.

"I wouldn't say that," Jack replied. "I can tell how much you cared for him."

She nodded, turning to him. "I did, but he—" Her confession was halted by the feel of Jack's hands on her shoulders. His intense gaze burned into hers. And then he kissed her. A sweet, simple kiss with none of the doubt and confusion that had tainted their encounter the previous evening.

In the end, she couldn't tell him. She just let him kiss her, there in the ruins of the old chapel. Perhaps she was afraid of the anger and recriminations that might follow her revelation. Or maybe it was simply a way to maintain a safe distance between them. She wasn't sure what it was. But when they walked back to Felicity, hand in hand, Jack Beaumont still believed that Maddie had been happily married to Lamar Parmentier.

MADDIE HAD THE KITCHEN all to herself and it was heaven. She'd given Calpurnia and Truett the evening off, claiming that Truett was spending so much extra time guarding Lamar that he deserved more hours to himself. When she'd told Calpurnia that she would take care of dinner, the cook had mumbled and shook her head.

If Calpurnia suspected what was going on between Maddie and Jack, she didn't come right out and say it. But from her ongoing mistrust of Jack to her surreptitious glares whenever she caught them in the same room, Maddie knew that their relationship was under close scrutiny.

Maddie stared at the package of fresh pasta she held in her hand. Their relationship. Was that what it was? The word sounded so generic, nothing like what had sprung up between them. They weren't lovers yet, but they were more than friends. They existed in an odd limbo of doubt and confusion, a place where she felt both content and restless at the same moment, a place in which the slightest mistake would have the capacity to destroy everything they had become.

Maddie wasn't even certain when it had started

Maybe that day in the stables, or the night before last, when he'd kissed her on the riverbank. Or perhaps it had all begun the day she'd walked into his office in San Francisco. All she really knew was that she'd made a spot for him in her life here at Felicity.

When he wasn't standing guard in the upstairs parlor, she found any number of excuses to be near him. And to her surprise, he seemed to enjoy her company as much as she did his. There were times when she would look up to find him staring at her, his gaze fixed on her face as if he were trying to see beyond her eyes and into her mind. At first she'd felt compelled to look away, paralyzed by nerves. But now she simply smiled and stared back into his blue eyes.

Maddie had never had a boyfriend. Sure, she'd dated occasionally, but she'd never met a man she could really talk to. Not the way she talked to Jack. Even though she had to keep so much of her life a secret from him, he still managed to draw her out, to ask her opinions and to contemplate her replies. But it wasn't all serious discussion, for he seemed to take great delight in teasing her until she laughed out loud.

Maddie was just about to whip up a shrimp étouffée for dinner when Jack came strolling through the kitchen. He'd been helping Jim Bob in the stables again, and his bare torso was shiny with perspiration. Maddie stared for a good long moment, admiring the play of muscles across his chest, the sinewy strength of his arms, the hard washboard abdomen. She wondered if there would ever come a time when she could touch him, indiscriminately and spontaneously.

"Are you cooking tonight?" he asked, grabbing a beer from the refrigerator.

"Um-hmm." She turned back to her sauté pan, determined to keep her mind on raw shellfish rather than his raw animal masculinity.

"I haven't eaten this good since..." Jack chuckled. "Come to think of it, I've never eaten this good."

"What would your mother say to that?" Maddie asked, moving to chop an onion.

"She would be forced to admit that you'd run circles around her in the kitchen. She's a meat-and-potatoes cook, after raising three boys and taking care of my dad. That's about all we would eat."

"Don't you cook for yourself?" Maddie asked, glancing over at him.

That brought a long laugh and a rueful shake of his head. "When I was in the navy, I ate fast food. In the field, MREs. I'm not sure I'd even know what to do in a kitchen, except maybe the dishes. But I'm great at ripping open plastic packages and takeout containers."

"What's an MRE?" Maddie asked.

"Meal ready to eat. The modern day version of K rations. So saturated with preservatives that if you buried one in the Iraqi sand you could dig it up in a hundred years and eat it. The only thing worth consuming was the candy."

"That sounds awful," Maddie said, wrinkling her nose. "It's bad enough to be so far away from home, fighting a war, but to put up with bad..." Maddie paused, realizing how ridiculous her words sounded.

"Food? You're right. Sometimes all I could think about was food and water. It kept your mind off the really bad things."

She shook her head. "Sometimes I take food a little too seriously. So, what did you eat?"

"My favorite was the chili macaroni, then the chicken and rice. Although whenever we were billeted near the French forces, we used to trade. Three of our MREs for one of their field meals."

"The French do have a way with food," Maddie said.

"Well, you've spoiled me. Back in 'Frisco I live on burgers and fries. I don't think I can ever enjoy fast food again after that gumbo you fed me the other night. I'll just have to starve, I guess."

Maddie grabbed him by the arm and pulled him up out of his chair. "No, you won't. I'm going to give you cooking lessons."

Jack's eyebrow quirked up and he wrapped his arms around her waist. "Yeah? You're going to be my teacher?"

She gave him a playful shove. "You can be my sous-chef. That's kind of like a first mate, I think. We'll start with a simple sauté. Tonight, Mr. Beaumont, you will make *my* dinner."

Maddie grabbed a kitchen towel from the drawer beside the sink. "Raise your arms," she ordered. When he did, she reached around him to tuck the towel into the waistband of his jeans.

"I think I like this cooking business," Jack said. "Can you do that again, only lower?"

Maddie cleared her throat. "I think we should stick to the subject, Monsieur Beaumont."

He leaned close, brushing her hair with his chin, trying to nuzzle her ear. "I thought we were doing just fine. I liked that…subject."

"I—I did, too."

"Then I'll make you a trade. You give me cooking lessons and I'll give you kissing lessons."

"I kiss just fine."

"Then touching lessons," he insisted.

"I don't need lessons," Maddie muttered, trying to

keep from staring at his mouth. That incredible mouth that worked such magic. The things that went through her mind when he kissed her, why, they were almost obscene! Shaking herself, she snatched up a sauté pan and a wooden spoon and handed them to him.

"We start with high heat," she said.

"I think I'm past that stage," Jack said.

"Put the pan on the stove," she ordered, wriggling out of his embrace. "Heat it, then add some of that olive oil."

She carefully led him through the steps of the étouffée, showing him how to chop vegetables and make a perfect nut-brown roux. At first, he teased and joked, but as the recipe became more complicated, he listened intently. He really was quite adept for an amateur.

As the étouffée simmered on the stove and the rice cooked, they wandered out to the porch swing on the verandah. Jack had grabbed a bottle of wine from the rack and poured each of them a glass, setting the bottle at his feet. "How did you learn to be such a good cook?" he asked.

"Chef," Maddie replied, taking a sip of the merlot. "I worked in restaurants. I studied in Paris." She didn't think twice before revealing herself. Perhaps she needed to let him in, to tell him the truth little by little. Then, when she told him the rest, it wouldn't be so overwhelming. "I'll have to teach you sauces. If you know sauces you can make an elegant dish out of very common ingredients."

"I know sauces," Jack said. "Barbecue, taco, Tabasco, Worcestershire, steak. Even the fancy ones like soy and teriyaki."

"Those aren't sauces, they're condiments. Béarnaise, béchamel, brown. Hollandaise, rémoulade and véloute. You could put hollandaise on top of an old sock and if the sauce was well made, it would be worth eating.''

"You've never tasted one of my socks," Jack said.

Maddie sighed impatiently. He really was impossible! She'd promised herself that they would have a serious discussion at the first possible moment. She'd tell him everything. But the time never seemed right. Whenever they were laughing, she didn't want to spoil a happy moment. And when they were at odds, she didn't want to make him angrier.

"All right," he conceded. "Someday you can teach me sauces."

"Yes, someday," Maddie repeated, a numbness seeping into her thoughts. She'd made an empty promise. To believe that she and Jack Beaumont would have a "someday" was pure folly. She'd hired him to guard her "dead husband." When the truth was finally revealed, he'd go back to where he'd come from and she would return to her life and her restaurant.

Maddie distractedly brushed her hands over the soft folds of her skirt. Maybe she shouldn't tell him at all. They could continue on as they had, enjoying the attraction that sparked between them, teasing and touching until they could no longer resist the inevitable.

And when it was all over, he would leave. And she would go back to her life. Clean and simple, with no regrets or recriminations. The more she thought about it, the more Maddie realized that it might be best to remain a widow. At least until Jackson Beaumont walked out of her life for good.

"I—I think the rice is done," she said, jumping up from beside him. "Maybe we should eat."

She retreated to the safety of the kitchen and the remainder of the dinner preparations. This was where she belonged, she told herself, with her stove and her pans and her recipes. She'd built a future at Delaney's, a future she'd been content with until just a few days ago. A future that didn't include a man.

Maddie snatched a spoon from the counter and pulled the cover off the pot of rice. She didn't *have* to fall in love with Jackson Beaumont—not if she didn't want to. She'd just put some of her characteristic determination to work.

After all, lust was a much safer alternative to love, wasn't it?

# 5

SHE HAD DISAPPEARED again. After their dinner of shrimp étouffée and the innocent good-night kiss they had shared, Jack had stupidly assumed that everything had changed between them. But after another long night passed in the parlor, he woke from a few hours sleep to find that Maddie was nowhere to be found.

Jack shook his head and gripped the steering wheel in white-knuckled hands, the wind whipping against his face as he sped south on the interstate. This time, Calpurnia wasn't at all forthcoming with an explanation, nor was the rest of Judge Parmentier's staff. Jack had the next thirty-six hours to himself, and he had wanted to spend every second of that time with Maddie.

His mind flashed back to an image of her standing in front of the crumbling chapel, the white blossoms from the crepe myrtles falling over her like snow. In that instant, he'd forgotten everything that had passed before—all his suspicions and doubts. He could almost feel her mouth beneath his, the sweet taste of her kiss.

Before, he'd been obsessed with learning the truth. Now he was beginning not to care. Whatever the truth was, it was in the past, wasn't it? When he thought of Maddie, he wanted to think about the present—and the future. Of long, lazy days spent talking, of endless nights in each other's arms.

He glanced over his shoulder, then smoothly pulled the car out to pass a rickety old pickup truck. The future. Until now, the future had loomed in front of him, a vast empty void to be filled with whatever life he managed to cobble together. Maddie had changed that. For the first time, he could imagine himself settled and satisfied. He could be happy with a woman like Maddie.

Jack's jaw tightened and he cursed softly. Could he really? As long as he suspected her of keeping secrets, he'd be a fool to invest any thoughts toward a future. Hell, he really didn't know who she was. He fixed his gaze on the road ahead, and the first exit sign for New Orleans flashed by.

Well, he could always find out, couldn't he? After all, wasn't that the real reason he'd decided to visit New Orleans? Though he might not want to admit it, there were too many questions left between them, and he needed answers. The sooner, the better.

He followed the highway as it skimmed the downtown area. Though he'd been to New Orleans only once in his life, he knew where he wanted to go first. He and Lucas Kincaid had spent a rowdy one-week leave in the French Quarter. They'd stayed up all night, every night, drinking and carousing, chasing skirts until they both could barely stand.

That seemed like a lifetime ago. Now Lucas was happily married, to a woman who had hired him as a bodyguard. When Jack had heard about the marriage, he'd jokingly said that Kincaid was the one who really needed protection. And now it was happening all over again. Jack had managed to find himself smitten with a beautiful client. Never mind that the body he was protecting was her dead husband's.

"Something about this job," he muttered, pulling off at the exit for the Vieux Carré. "Throw a needy woman in a navy man's path and he turns into a damn knight in shining armor."

The French Quarter was exactly as he'd remembered it—exotic and a little seedy. He parked the car in a public lot on Canal Street near the river, then walked up toward Jackson Square. He'd grab a quick breakfast, then head over to the courthouse and get to work.

The streets were surprisingly quiet, offering a respite of redemption after a long night of sin. The bars and jazz clubs were closed to patrons, though some owners stood out in front washing the sidewalks, jukebox Dixieland drifting out from the dark interiors. Bakers, working with wood-fired ovens, offered baguettes and buttery croissants. And a few tourists snapped pictures from the narrow sidewalks, enchanted with the pretty pastel-painted buildings and the intriguing porte cocheres that hid secret courtyard gardens.

Jack purchased a croissant and a cup of strong black coffee from a bakery, then strolled the narrow streets. He glanced up at lacy wrought-iron balconies, some filled with plants and flowers, others with residents still dressed in their robes, reading the morning paper. The French Quarter was nothing like he'd remembered, although he and Kincaid had never seen it in broad daylight or completely sober.

Jackson Square was an oasis of green in the midst of the densely situated buildings in the Quarter. A trio of young street musicians played a raucous ragtime tune just outside the wrought-iron fence and a unicyclist carefully balanced as he twirled a fire baton. The

French Market beckoned from the riverfront, and Jack wandered in that direction as he finished his coffee, through the colonnaded arcade of shops and restaurants to the open-air produce stands on the far end.

Hawkers shouted of the beauties of their vegetables and fruits and fish. Jack paid for an apple, rubbing it on his shirt as he turned away from a toothless fruit vendor. He stared through the crowd of shoppers and then froze when he caught a flash of a familiar face.

"Maddie," he murmured. Pushing through the press of people, he started in her direction, but she disappeared as quickly as she had materialized. When he reached the spot where she had stood, he scanned the crowd. But no one resembling Maddie could be seen.

Jack furrowed his hand through his hair and chuckled softly. "You're imagining things," he muttered. "You're so obsessed with the woman, you see her everywhere you look." Hell, he was in a produce market; Maddie was an excellent chef. It was no wonder he imagined her here.

Satisfied with his rationalization, he bit into the apple, then glanced at his watch. A call to the agency was probably in order, since his last call had been three days ago. Besides, he could find out where Mark had gone to do the background checks on the judge's employees. If Jack dug a little deeper, he was sure to find the truth about Maddie.

Jack hadn't brought his cell phone, so he found a pay phone nearby. As he waited for his credit card call to go through, he picked up the phone book and idly flipped to the page that listed Parmentier. He shouldn't have been surprised to find Lamar listed, but he was.

"Prytania Street," he said, hanging up the phone before Charilyn had the chance to answer. A map in the front of the phone book gave him the location of the judge's home in the city's Garden District. A friendly vendor gave him directions. Before long, Jack had hopped onto a streetcar on Canal Street and was heading upriver.

The change in scenery was startling. Leaving the French Creole influences of the Vieux Carré, the car ran through the business district first, then the warehouse district with its unusual art museum, and into a beautiful neighborhood filled with lush gardens and well-kept antebellum town houses. He jumped off at First Street and quickly found the address he'd scribbled from the phone book.

An elegant iron fence surrounded the property. Two gnarled live oaks, draped with shreds of Spanish moss, hid the overgrown front garden and Italianate mansion from all but the most interested pedestrians. Like Felicity, the town house boasted deep galleries on both the first and second floor.

Jack approached the front gate, but found it locked. The tall shutters were drawn on both floors of the house, which looked utterly abandoned. He considered jumping the fence. Any SEAL worth his salt would be able to break into the house, get a good look inside and get out without being detected. Jack glanced around, ready to boost himself up and over the pointed iron bars. Then he realized he wasn't alone.

An elderly woman stared at him from the adjoining property, her muddy forearms resting on the fence, her casual clothes smudged with dirt. "There's no one home," she called.

"I was looking for Mrs. Parmentier," Jack said.

The woman's eyebrows shot up in surprise beneath

her wide-brimmed straw hat. "Sarah? Oh my, she passed on nearly thirty years ago."

Jack shook his head. "No, I'm looking for the judge's second wife."

The woman chuckled, taken aback by his statement. "The judge never remarried. He's still pinin' after Sarah—or was, until he passed on, poor man. Now there was a match. When she went on to her reward we all knew there'd never be another woman in his life. Thirty years. That's a long time to be alone. They're together now."

"Are you sure?" Jack asked. "She's young and pretty. Dark hair. She supposedly lived here with the judge."

"I've lived here all my life, young man. I know everyone *and* their business on this particular block of Prytania Street. I'd know if there was a new lady livin' in that house. Besides the servants and a few close friends of the judge's, that old house has been quiet since Sarah died." The woman's expression grew wistful. "Oh, she used to throw some fine parties, Sarah did."

Jack cursed beneath his breath. Just when he thought he'd figured this whole mess out, some new revelation popped up to throw him into confusion again. He had nearly resigned himself to the fact that Maddie was indeed the judge's wife and that she loved the old man and couldn't possibly have anything to do with his death.

But now that presumption would have to be carefully reexamined. If she wasn't the judge's widow, who the hell was she? "Thanks," Jack finally said. "I appreciate the information."

"Real sad about the judge," the woman called. "We haven't heard a thing about the funeral. I s'pose they buried him up at Felicity. You wouldn't know, would you?"

Jack shrugged, then gave her a wave, unwilling to provide any more details regarding the judge's death. Hell, he hadn't managed to put the details in the proper order yet himself, and he'd been living with the judge's most trusted companions...if they were to be trusted, he mused.

"I'm getting damn tired of playing detective," he muttered as he started back toward St. Charles Avenue. "I was hired to be a bodyguard. I should guard my body and mind my own business."

He walked nearly three blocks before he realized that he was headed in the wrong direction. The tall brick walls of Lafayette Cemetery loomed large to his left, across busy Washington Avenue. To the right, a block away, a streetcar rumbled past, its bell clanging.

Jack turned toward the streetcar stop, but a fleeting image caught his eye and he froze. It was Maddie again! An oath burst from his lips and he pressed the heel of his hand to his forehead. What was wrong with him? He was acting like a man completely besotted!

He pinched his eyes closed, then looked again. But to his surprise, she hadn't disappeared. The woman continued to walk down Washington Avenue, away from him and from the streetcar stop. It didn't take him long to decide to follow her.

She walked at a quick pace, but Jack had no trouble keeping up. From the back, she certainly looked like Maddie. He had admired the gentle sway of Maddie's hips enough times to recognize her walk, though the dress she wore didn't look familiar. Jack maintained a safe distance, staying close to the high walls of the cemetery and later in the shade of trees and fences. If

Maddie was in New Orleans, why hadn't she stopped at the town house?

He watched the woman turn down Magazine Street, catching a brief profile in the distance. If it wasn't Maddie, the woman he was following could have been her sister. He hurried, but when he got to the corner, she was gone.

"Damn," he muttered. Had she seen him and suspected that she was being followed? He quickly walked halfway up the block. A brief flicker of movement caught his eye. He stared in the direction of a small town house set near the next corner, its exterior stucco painted a pale peach. Its front door slammed shut and he thought he saw the curtains flutter. A sign on the fence identified the place as a restaurant. "Delaney's," he murmured. Maybe she'd gone inside for lunch.

The restaurant was one of several public places along the block she could have entered. There were a few shops on the other side of Magazine Street, but he would have seen her cross. Jack stepped through the open gate and took the front steps two at a time. He grinned when the door of the restaurant opened. She'd be surprised to see him, but certainly she'd invite him to dine with her. He couldn't imagine a more pleasant way to spend the afternoon.

The foyer of the old town house was elegantly appointed, a crystal chandelier glittering in the midday sun that poured through the fanlight above the door. Plush Oriental rugs covered the plank floors and soft muted tones of color washed the walls and ornate plasterwork. On one side of the foyer was a dining room, set with ten or twelve tables. On the other side, a paneled library served as the bar area, with addi-

# PLAY THE Lucky Key Game and get

## HOW TO PLAY:

1. With a coin, carefully scratch off gold area at the right. Then check the claim chart to se what we have for you — **FREE BOOKS** and a **FREE GIFT** — **ALL YOURS FREE!**

2. Send back this card and you'll receive brand-new Harlequin Temptation® novels. These books have a cover price of $4.25 each, but they are yours to keep absolutely free.

3. There's no catch. You're under no obligation to buy anything. We charge nothing — ZERO — for your first shipment. And you don't have to make any minimum number o purchases — not even one!

4. The fact is thousands of readers enjoy receiving books by mail from the Harlequin Reader Service® months before they're available in stores. They like the convenience of home delivery and they love our discount prices!

5. We hope that after receiving your free books you'll want to remain a subscriber. But the choice is yours — to continue or cancel, any time at all! So why not take us up on our invitation, with no risk of any kind. You'll be glad you did!

# YOURS FREE!
## A SURPRISE MYSTERY GIFT

We can't tell you what it is...but we're sure you'll like it! A
## FREE GIFT—
just for playing the LUCKY KEY game!

# FREE GIFTS!

## PLAY THE
### Lucky Key Game

Scratch gold area with a coin.
Then check below to see the gifts you get!

**YES!** I have scratched off the gold area. Please send me all the gifts for which I qualify. I understand I am under no obligation to purchase any books, as explained on the back and on the opposite page.

**342 HDL CH9R**

Name
_____
(PLEASE PRINT CLEARLY)

Address _____ Apt.#

City _____ Prov. _____ Postal Code

| | |
|---|---|
| 🔑🔑🔑🔑 2 free books plus a mystery gift | 🔑🔑🔑 1 free book |
| 🔑🔑🔑 2 free books | 🔑🔑 Try Again! |

# The Harlequin Reader Service™ — Here's how it works:

Accepting free books places you under no obligation to buy anything. You may keep the books and gift and return the shipping statement marked "cancel." If you do not cancel, about a month later we'll send you 4 additional novels, and bill you just $3.57 each, plus 25¢ delivery per book and GST.* That's the complete price — and compared to cover prices of $4.25 each — quite a bargain! You may cancel at any time, but if you choose to continue, every month we'll send you 4 more books, which you may either purchase at the discount price...or return to us and cancel your subscription.

*Terms and prices subject to change without notice.
Canadian residents will be charged applicable provincial taxes and GST.

HARLEQUIN READER SERVICE
PO BOX 609
FORT ERIE ON    L2A 9Z9

019561919199-L2A5X3-BR01

MAIL▶POSTE
Canada Post Corporation/Société canadienne des postes
Postage paid    Port payé
If mailed in Canada    si posté au Canada

Business    Réponse
Reply    d'affaires

01956199199    01

tional tables. To his surprise, there wasn't a single patron in the restaurant, even though it was nearly noon.

"I'm sorry, sir. We're not open for lunch on Mondays."

Jack turned to see an attractive young woman approach from the rear of the house. "But I just saw someone...a woman." He glanced around again. He could have sworn Maddie had come inside. But the place was empty.

"I've been here since ten and we've had no customers. Were you perhaps supposed to meet someone here?"

"No, I was..." He couldn't say he'd been following someone. That would sound too bizarre, frightening even.

"I could make a reservation for you for another time," she offered. "We're open for lunch tomorrow. And there's dinner tonight. We'll be having a wonderful veal topped with crab and hollandaise sauce. Our soup is crayfish bisque. And our dessert special is crème brûlée with a fresh Chambord sauce."

"No," Jack said, frowning. "It sounds great, but I'm not going to be staying in town."

"We also serve a Sunday brunch," she added.

He shook his head, took one last look around, then slipped out the front door. With a sigh, he plopped down on the top step and scrubbed at his face with his hands. He'd managed to waste an entire morning in New Orleans, chasing a figment of his imagination.

Had he become so crazy for Maddie Parmentier that he saw her wherever he turned? Was he so suspicious of her that he imagined some evasiveness and deceit in every move she made, every word she uttered?

"You're going to make yourself nuts if you try to figure this woman out," Jack murmured. "Just do your damn job. Watch the coffin and leave the widow alone."

Though the plan sounded great in theory, Jack knew it would be hard to put into practice. After all that had passed between them, both the good and the bad, he knew it would be nearly impossible to stay away from Maddie Parmentier.

"Is HE STILL OUT THERE?" Maddie asked.

Anne Ladret peered through the lace curtains and nodded, her pale blond hair falling across her eyes. "He's just sitting there."

"What's he doing?"

Anne sighed in exasperation. "Why don't you go out there and find out? He's loitering on the front steps of your restaurant. If you don't want him there, call the cops."

Maddie shook her head. "I don't want him to know I'm here."

"Then you want me to call the cops?"

Maddie shook her head. "I don't want him arrested. I just want him...gone."

"Who is this guy? An ex-boyfriend you're trying to avoid? A current boyfriend you're playing mind games with? Hey, if you don't want him, I'll take him. He's cute!"

"Never mind who or what he is," Maddie said. "I have to get out of here." She grabbed Anne's hand and dragged her toward the front door. The manager of Delaney's was a good friend and could be trusted to be discreet. "Lock the door. We'll sneak out through the kitchen."

"We?" Anne asked.

"We'll take my car. It's parked out back. You'll drive and I'll hide on the floor. Once we turn up

Washington, you can get out and walk back to the restaurant and I'll drive on to Felicity."

"You know, ever since you and your friends
hatched this scheme with Lamar, you've been acting
very strange."

Maddie drew in a deep breath. She had told Anne
everything, right down to the very last detail—that is,
everything except what had been happening between
her and Jack Beaumont. If Maddie was going to be
away from the restaurant for any length of time, she
needed the full support of her manager. Anne kept the
kitchen running smoothly and watched over Maddie's two sous-chefs. Anne kept the books and made
the bank deposits. Anne had been a real trooper, until
now.

"I have to get back to Felicity," Maddie said. "Before *he* does. Now, are you going to help me?"

"He's at Felicity?" Anne asked. "Staying there, with
you?"

"He's the guy I hired to guard Lamar."

"He knows that Lamar is alive?"

"No, he's guarding Lamar's coffin."

Anne peeked out the curtains once more, then
sighed as she locked the front door. "What a perfect
waste of a good-looking man."

Maddie grasped her arm. "Stop drooling. I just had
the rugs cleaned." She dragged Anne back through
the kitchen, grabbing her books and her bag along the
way. She scribbled a few more notes for the chefs, then
motioned her friend out the back door and into the
waiting car.

To Maddie's great relief, she made her escape without detection, though Anne did send Jack a little wave
as they passed by. "He is adorable. What did you say
his name was?"

"I didn't say," Maddie muttered, squished beneath the seat and the dash. "Now, I want you to go back to the restaurant, but make sure he doesn't see you. Let yourself in the back door, then call me on the car phone. We still need to go over the menus for this week and I want to discuss the liquor order. Oh, and David found a new wine he wanted to add to the list. And—"

"Don't worry," Anne said. "We've been doing fine so far. You've trained your sous-chefs well. The customers haven't even noticed that you're not in the kitchen."

"Maybe I've trained them too well," Maddie muttered. "If they get too cocky, they'll quit and open their own restaurant down the street."

"They'd never leave," Anne said. "They worship the ground you walk on, the air you breathe, the pots and pans you throw at them."

Maddie pushed herself up from the floor and looked out the window. "All right, you can pull over."

Anne found a place at the curb and hopped out while Maddie slid into the driver's seat. "Remember," Maddie warned. "If he's still sitting on the front steps, don't let him see you. And call me as soon as you get back."

Anne waved as she pulled away. Maddie had barely reached the interstate before her car phone rang. To her relief, Jack had stopped loitering and was now gone from the front steps of Delaney's.

She spent the ninety-minute drive between New Orleans and Felicity carefully reviewing the menus for the restaurant. When she'd finished with Anne, Maddie held a long conference call with Dave and Phil, her assistant chefs. It was nearly impossible to run a kitchen from the front seat of a car, but she had no choice. She was needed at Felicity. A few scorched sauces and an overcooked fish or two was a small price to pay for protecting Lamar.

But how much longer would this go on? Lamar had promised that if he hadn't been able to find the person who had attempted to kill him within a week, he'd reveal the truth about his "death." He had been certain the killer would come back to be sure the job had been completed. But they were going on day ten since the poisoning.

Maddie was beginning to have her doubts. What if the man was long gone? She could only keep up the charade for so long. People were going to start calling for a funeral, and she'd have no choice but to "bury" Lamar.

None of this really made sense to her. From the start, she'd insisted that Lamar go to the police for protection. But he and Dilby had cooked up this ridiculous plan, then pulled her into it for reasons she couldn't begin to explain. There would be hell to pay when the truth finally came out, considering all the suffering the judge had caused his good friends and neighbors.

"There *will* be hell to pay," Maddie murmured as she swung the car off the interstate and onto the highway that led to Fells Crossing. "And some of it will come from me."

She covered the twenty miles between Baton Rouge and Felicity in record time. Dust and gravel flew from the tires of her car as she raced up the drive and screeched to a halt. Jack's rental car was nowhere to be seen. Emile came shuffling around the corner of the house and she tossed him her keys as she hurried up the front steps. Calpurnia was waiting at the door.

"You're movin' as fast as a kerosene cat in hell with

gasoline drawers on," Calpurnia said. "Somethin' must be up."

"He saw me," Maddie said, closing the front door behind her and leaning against it. "He was in New Orleans."

"Who?"

"Jack. He was at the restaurant. Somehow, he saw me. He must have gone to the town house, or maybe he knows all about me. He found out. How could he have found out? You didn't tell him, did you?"

Calpurnia shook her head, wiping her hands on her apron. She slipped an arm around Maddie's waist and drew her toward the kitchen. "What's got you so bothered up? Tell the man the truth. Lamar said you could. Then you wouldn't have to be runnin' around like a fool."

"No!" Maddie snapped. "I—I can't."

"Why not?"

"Because it will just complicate things," she said, her breath coming in short gasps. "As soon as we figure out who tried to kill Lamar, it will be all over. Jack will go back to San Francisco and everything will get back to normal."

"And you're just goin' to let him believe that you and Lamar are married? Even when Lamar comes back to life?"

"He'll be gone before Lamar rises from the dead. He won't need to know the truth."

Calpurnia pushed her down in one of the kitchen chairs, then fetched her a glass of cold lemonade. "But you aren't married to Lamar," she countered. "You're a single woman without a man. Is that what you're so afraid he'll find out?"

"No," Maddie said.

"I think it is," Calpurnia said. "You're afraid that if

he knows that, he might just start wantin' you more than he already does. And you're keeping Lamar's death in your pocket like your ace in the hole. If things get too serious for you, you just put on your widow's weeds again. That'll surely send Jack Beaumont back to where he came from." Calpurnia reached out and patted Maddie's shoulder. "Honey, when are you goin' to give yourself some credit? That man has got eyes for you. And I can see you don't mind him lookin'."

"So? That doesn't mean I'm falling in love with him."

"Would that be the worst thing in the world?" Calpurnia asked in a tender voice. "You deserve a good man, a man that will watch over you and treat you right. Jackson Beaumont seems to be a good man, Maddie Delaney. And I'm the last one to admit I might have been wrong about him."

"Good men don't marry petty criminals," Maddie said, her words cold as the ice that clinked in her glass.

She had tried to tell herself over and over that he could accept the real truth about her. Not just about Lamar, but about her past, for that was tangled up in this whole mess as tightly as anything else. As long as she told him in the right way, at the right time.

But when she thought about her past and compared it to the life he'd lived, she just couldn't make the two fit. They were like puzzle pieces, only from entirely different puzzles. She was hiding a lie behind another lie. That's why she couldn't tell him about the judge. It was much easier to spin out this story of his "death" and her "widowhood" than to let Jack get closer to her.

His visit to Delaney's had sent up walls all around her, and though she wanted to be honest with him, she had to face the fact that protecting her own heart was more important than capturing his. During her life on the streets, she'd learned to look out for number one, and she had to do that now.

"Why do you have to tell him about all that?" Calpurnia asked. "It's in your past and none of it was your fault. You did what you had to do. You more than any of us."

"That doesn't make it right, Calpurnia." She drew in a long breath, then laughed softly. "Hey, maybe I won't even have to tell him. He was at Delaney's. He's a smart man, he can put two and two together. He's probably already figured out who I am and he's checking my record right now. He'll be on his way back to San Francisco before the sun sets."

"You don't know that."

Maddie sighed and started toward the stairs. "When he gets back, tell him I was in Baton Rouge shopping. Tell him that I'm taking a nap and can't be disturbed. I—I don't want to talk to him. Not now."

JACK DIDN'T GET BACK to Felicity until nearly nine. After strolling a five-block section of Magazine Street, looking into every shop and restaurant, he could only conclude that he'd been mistaken—about the woman at the French Market, the woman in the Garden District. And most importantly, about the intriguing woman who lived at Felicity.

She wasn't married to Lamar Parmentier. A thorough search of the court records hadn't turned up a single shred of proof. Nor had a casual questioning of the judge's courthouse staff. They all seemed terribly upset by the judge's death and completely unaware of the existence of a second Mrs. Parmentier.

Jack did gain one interesting insight from the

judge's secretary, an elderly woman who had worked in Lamar's office for nearly thirty years. She mentioned Sarah, but in the same sentence told Jack how, after his wife's death, Lamar had dedicated his energies to helping the less fortunate. Jack had assumed she meant charity work. But the secretary went on to explain that the judge had taken in an "unsavory element."

"Right into his home!" she had confided in a stunned whisper. "Actual criminals. We all thought it was unwise, but Judge Lamar believed in the good in everyone he met. He was so trusting, so generous."

So Jack had been forced back to square one, back to his earlier suspicions that Maddie and her little troupe had indeed been involved in the judge's death. As he wandered through the French Quarter, listening half-heartedly to the music spilling out of the bars and clubs, he'd gone over it all in his mind again and again. They had all conspired to swindle Lamar's legitimate heirs out of his estate. And they'd managed to suck the local law-enforcement officer into their scheme. Dilby was as dirty as yesterday's laundry.

If only Jack could get a look at Lamar's will—that would be the key. If the will had been changed recently, the changes could very well implicate Maddie. Jack winced inwardly. The honor-bound streak in him, the code that he'd built his navy career around, told him he had to expose the truth. Yet deep inside, he still wanted to believe her, even after every bit of truth told him otherwise.

Maybe that had been the judge's mistake. Like Jack, Lamar had been captivated by her beauty. He'd believed that Maddie was worth loving, when all along she'd been weaving a web of deceit and betrayal. It had cost Lamar Parmentier his life. If Jack allowed his feelings to override his common sense, it might cost him just as dearly. It might cost him his heart and his soul.

The house was quiet when he slipped inside. They hadn't waited dinner. The dining room was dark, the tall French doors closed to the evening breeze. Jack stopped in the kitchen and grabbed a cold bottle of beer, then glanced at the schedule posted on the refrigerator. Truett had the late watch tonight. Jack was scheduled for a double shift tomorrow, from 5:00 a.m. until 10:00 p.m., then had the following day and evening off.

He wandered back through the butler's pantry and the dining room and started up the stairs to his bedroom. But a sound from the library caused him to pause. With quiet steps, he changed direction and listened through the door of the library. Maddie was inside, and she was having a rather heated discussion with someone. Determined not to be tricked again, Jack grabbed the doorknob and flung the door open.

But he didn't find a strange man inside the library. Nor did he find Maddie alone. She and Calpurnia, stunned by the sudden intrusion, stared at him from behind a book-filled library table.

"You're back," Maddie finally said, her eyes wide.

"I'm back," he repeated, his gaze fixed on hers.

They stared at each other for a long time, Jack transfixed by her beauty. The color in her cheeks was high and her hair tumbled around her face. She wore a pretty silk robe, this one different from the one he'd seen before. It nearly covered her bare feet, but revealed the perfect amount of cleavage. He fought the urge to walk across the room and pull her into his arms, to push aside the robe and take pleasure in the feel of her body beneath his hands.

"Yep, he's back," Calpurnia said. "We're clear on that point, now, aren't we."

Maddie glanced over at the cook and forced a smile. "I can finish this on my own, Calpurnia. Why don't you go and keep Truett company? I think he's listening to the ball game on the radio."

Calpurnia gave them both a once-over, then muttered something beneath her breath as she bustled out of the room. When the door slammed behind her, Jack slowly sauntered to the judge's desk and took a seat in the huge leather chair. He leaned back and swung both feet up to rest on the edge of the rosewood desk.

Maddie watched him warily, the smile still frozen on her flushed face. "Did you have a pleasant day?" she asked.

He took a long drink of his beer, then shrugged. "It was a very...illuminating day."

She turned her attention back to dusting a leather-bound book. "Where did you go?"

"New Orleans," he replied. "And you?"

She seemed bothered by his question and cleared her throat before she spoke. "Baton Rouge. I went shopping." She drew a deep breath. "You missed dinner. I made a lovely veal dish. Veal is never good warmed up."

"I grabbed something before I left New Orleans." Jack sighed, then leaned back again. "So, I see you're getting rid of a few of the judge's things."

"What?" Maddie blinked in surprise. "No. Why would you say that?"

He pointed to the cardboard box on the end of the library table. "You're packing."

"The judge wanted to donate these to the library at Tulane. He told me...before he died."

Jack pushed up from the chair and circled the desk,

never taking his eyes off of her. She squirmed beneath his gaze, her hands fluttering over the books in an attempt to look nonchalant. "I suppose you'll have to clear his things out sooner or later. I mean, Felicity is yours now. You're a very wealthy woman. What are you going to do with all that money?"

She gaped at him, her expression filled with disbelief. "I—I can't believe you're asking me this."

He leaned back against the edge of the desk. "Come on, Maddie. We're friends, aren't we? It's a logical question. Practical, even. Are you going to travel? Buy yourself a little place down in the Caribbean? Maybe jet off to Paris for the fashion shows?"

"Don't be ridiculous," she murmured. "Besides, what I do is none of your business."

"But we're friends."

"A friend would never ask such questions."

Jack chuckled, then slowly crossed the room and sat on the table near her chair. "Maybe you're right. After all, what do we really know about each other? For instance, I don't know how you feel about politics—the national debt, foreign policy…crime."

Her hands stilled on the book she held, her knuckles going white. "Crime?"

"Yeah. Criminals. People who break the law. Why don't we start there. How do you feel about criminals, Maddie?"

"I suppose criminals are a bad thing," she began. "But then, I think you have to look at the circumstances surrounding their crime."

"Are you saying that it's sometimes all right to break the law?"

"Yes," she snapped. "I—I mean, no. It's not right, but sometimes circumstances make it…necessary…to survive."

Jack pondered her answer for a long moment, allowing her a little more time to squirm. "So what would those circumstances be?"

She stiffened, then turned to him, her eyes flashing anger. "Tell me, Mr. Beaumont, have you ever killed a man?"

The question took Jack by complete surprise. He had never felt comfortable talking about the dark side of his career as a Navy SEAL. And it was dark, this cold and calculated side of his being, the part of him that could take a man's life without even blinking. "It's not the same as murder," he said.

"And why is that?"

"Because the circum—" His jaw clenched and he cursed silently. How had she managed to turn this back on him? Now *he* was on the defensive. "It's different," he finally said.

She nodded slowly. "Maybe. We're all forced to make choices, aren't we? Good or bad. But sometimes we have no choice at all."

She gave him a sideways glance, and in her eyes he saw complete understanding, a steely strength glittering in the green depths that told him without words that she accepted him for who he was. She accepted all the things he'd done in his life in the name of honor and country. He'd always thought he'd have to keep that part of himself a secret. But now it lay exposed in front of her.

"No choice," he muttered.

Suddenly, in a rush of pure release, he felt all the guilt flood out of him. She understood; there was no need to explain. He'd never thought he'd find a woman who could comprehend that dark part of his life. But then, Maddie had her own demons, didn't she? And if he truly cared about her, then he would have to accept her for who she was, the same way she accepted him.

With a soft oath, Jack slid off the edge of the table. An instant later, he had her face cupped in his palms, her startled gaze turned up to his. And then his lips met hers. He expected her to resist, to haul off and slap him across the face. But she didn't. Instead, she matched his passion without reserve, wrapping her arms around his neck and opening her mouth beneath his.

Her tongue danced around his, urgent, demanding, offering a tantalizing prelude to what they might share. Jack groaned and pulled her nearer, until her soft breasts were pressed against his chest. She felt so delicate in his arms, and for a moment he thought to temper his desire. But then she raked her nails down his back, sending a shiver skittering along his spine.

This was no hothouse orchid, pampered by fawning care. He held a rose of exquisite beauty, tenacious beneath both the hot sun and icy wind, petal-soft yet thorn-sharpened. She would bend beneath his hand, but she wouldn't break. And if he pushed too hard, she might draw blood.

Jack slipped his fingers into the front of her robe and gently parted the silk. It slid back, revealing the thin fabric of her nightgown. His hands drifted over the gentle swell of her hips, the perfect curve of her backside. He pulled her against him, her soft belly meeting his hard desire.

The blood pounded in his head and he felt his heart race. And then she drew her hands along his back and slowly tugged the shirt from the waistband of his jeans. Her hands slipped inside, warm against his skin, skimming the shirt up until his chest lay bare to her eyes. Then she lowered her head and nuzzled against him, kissing and teasing, exploring with her tongue until she found his nipple.

Jack tipped his head back and drew in a sharp breath. For an instant, he felt as if he might pass out. Was this how it felt, to want a woman so badly that he'd be willing to die to possess her? He'd wondered how Maddie might have killed her husband with sex. It was quite clear that the notion was entirely possible.

With a low growl, Jack bent down and scooped her into his arms, capturing her mouth again. He carried her over to the long leather couch and carefully laid her down. And then he knelt over her, bracing his arms on either side of her head.

"Jack, I—"

He placed his finger over her lips. "Don't talk."

She pulled his hand away and wove her fingers through his. "We have to talk," she said.

"Nothing you say now makes any difference. It won't stop me from wanting you…from wanting this."

"It might," she murmured. "It will."

"Then I don't want to hear it," he said, hovering over her lips, desperate to taste her again. "The truth doesn't matter. Not now."

She stared at him, an uneasy expression worrying her delicate features. A tiny trace of apprehension glittered in her gaze. "This isn't right," she said. "We can't do this. Not until we're honest with each other."

Jack's jaw clenched and he cursed under his breath. What did she expect from him? Did she really believe that he could make love to her *after* she admitted the truth, *after* she confessed to murdering her husband? He wanted to believe the best of her and refused to acknowledge anything else. He was giving her an easy way out. "I don't want to hear the truth."

"You have to," Maddie said. "If you don't, then this ends right here."

He stared at her for a long moment, then pushed away from her and got to his feet. Shaking his head, he turned away and stared out the open French doors. "Then go," he said. "Now, before we say things we can't take back."

"But why?" Maddie asked. "I—I think you already know what I'm going to say."

"That doesn't mean I want to hear it."

She slowly crawled off the sofa and moved to his side. Hesitantly, she reached up to touch him, but he evaded her hand. "I thought you would understand," she said.

"I can't," he murmured, refusing to look at her.

With a soft sigh, she dropped her hand to her side and started for the door. At the last minute, she turned. A rueful smile curved her lips as she pulled her robe together and retied it. "I don't blame you. There are times when I can't forget what I was—what I am. How can I expect someone else to?"

With that, she turned and walked out of the library, closing the door softly behind her. Jack stood frozen in place for a long time, wishing her back in his arms. But he knew he shouldn't want her. She'd as much as admitted what she'd done. He pinched his eyes shut and cursed out loud.

Damn her. And damn him for being stupid enough to fall in love with her.

# 6

"TELL HIM THE TRUTH."

Maddie stared out at the river, watching as the sun dipped low in the sky. The horizon burned with fire, pink and orange streaks hanging over the marshy riverbank and the opposite shore. Cattails swayed against the gentle current and a red-winged blackbird trilled in the heavy heat of the late afternoon. "He knows," Maddie said, glancing over at Lamar.

The judge's white hair ruffled in the wind. He cut an imposing figure, standing with his back to the setting sun. She thought back to their early days together, to his absolute and unwavering faith in her goodness. And to her growing respect for him.

"All of it?" he asked.

She shrugged, wrapping her arms around herself. "All that really matters. He saw me in New Orleans yesterday and followed me to Delaney's. He must have had one of the people at his agency check up on me. I'm pretty sure he knows about my past."

The judge reached out and touched her elbow. "How?"

"Easy. He got a look at my records. I was quite the youthful offender, as you remember. Juvie was like my second home."

"Madeline, he couldn't have seen your records. They're sealed."

Maddie turned to Lamar, her eyes wide with bewilderment. "I don't understand."

The judge placed his hands on her shoulders. "Even if he wanted to find out about your past, he couldn't. When I took you in, I petitioned the court to have your records sealed. If you stayed out of trouble until age eighteen, the records would never see the light of day."

Tears suddenly swam in the corners of Maddie's eyes and she gave Lamar a wavering smile. "Thank you," she murmured, pressing her fingers to her trembling lips. "But I'm afraid that doesn't change anything. He suspects me of hiding something. You should have seen him. He was like a cat with a mouse. He had me backed into a corner and there was no way out."

"If he doesn't know what you've done, what does he *think* you've done?"

She stepped away and walked closer to the edge of the river. A frog jumped from the muddy bank into the water, a soft plop sending ripples toward the shore. "I don't know. Maybe he still thinks I murdered you."

Lamar gasped. "What?"

Maddie turned back to him and laughed. "It's true. He heard some rumor around town that I had something to do with your death. That I'd caused it."

"He thinks *you* poisoned me?"

"Not poison. Sex," Maddie said. "He thinks I killed you in the bedroom. I suspect this story is at least partly Eulalie's doing. She's does have a vivid imagination."

This brought an even more startled gasp from the judge, and a caustic oath. Maddie blinked, astonished at the judge's outburst. In all the time she'd known him, he'd always had such control over his temper. "Eulalie Rose Peavy," he muttered, his white eyebrows knitted into a scowl.

Maddie waved her hand and shook her head. "I know, I know. Don't ask me where she got the idea. Or why Jack Beaumont believes it."

"You have to tell him the truth, Madeline. You can't allow him to think these things about you. When he knows the truth, he'll love you as we do."

Maddie withdrew an envelope from the pocket in her skirt and held it up. "No, he won't. He made it very clear how he feels about criminals. I can't change my past, Lamar. I am what I am. And if I love him, I'd have to tell him."

"Do you love him, Madeline?"

"No," she said, her reply more instinct than truth. "And since I don't, I don't have to tell him anything. I just have to give him this."

"What is it?"

"His return ticket to San Francisco. I'm going to tell him that I've planned the funeral for Friday. And that I don't need his help anymore. He can leave in the morning and then everything will be back to normal."

"Except I'll still be dead," Lamar said.

"Sheriff Dilby stopped by before breakfast. He thinks that whoever tried to murder you is well satisfied that they did the job right. They're not coming back, at least not until you've risen from the grave. So, as soon as Jack Beaumont leaves Louisiana, we can set the record straight." She slipped the plane ticket back into her pocket. "And we can finally get that awful coffin out of your upstairs parlor."

Lamar frowned and tapped a finger over his lips as he considered what she'd told him. "Call Dilby," he finally said, "and tell him I want to see him. Tonight."

"Don't worry, Lamar. He promised me that after the truth came out, he'd get you protection. He said he'll even call in the FBI if you want. He'll find who tried to kill you."

"I'm sure he will," Lamar said distractedly. "But where will that leave you?"

"Relieved," Maddie said, not sure she understood his question. "We'll all be relieved once you're safe."

Lamar shook his head wearily. "Madeline, you know what I'm talking about. I can see you care about this man. And I can see how you're doing everything you can to avoid facing those feelings. Don't let love slip away. It's so very hard to find."

"I don't love him," Maddie insisted. As soon as the words left her lips, she was suddenly certain they were a lie. "I don't," she added, in an effort to convince herself.

"And I don't believe you," Lamar said. "Give yourself a chance at happiness, Madeline. You deserve it."

Maddie reached out and took his hand, rubbing papery-thin skin below his wrist. This man was so dear to her. From the time he'd found her, she'd lived her life to make him proud. "You don't have to worry about me," she said. "I'll be just fine." She gave his hand a squeeze and then forced a bright smile. "Now, I better go find Jack. He should be just about done baby-sitting that silly old coffin."

Maddie brushed a kiss on the judge's cheek, then started back toward the house. She didn't want to face Jack, especially after what had happened between them the night before. But now that she'd decided to put an end to everything they had shared, she felt free again, unencumbered by her past. Though she had let herself dream a little, though she'd fantasized a future with Jack, she was doing the practical thing. She'd put him out of her life, quickly and painlessly.

As she walked through the garden, she looked up to find him standing on the lower gallery watching her, his shoulder braced against one of the tall columns. She smiled hesitantly. For a moment he paused, then straightened and walked toward her, his gaze wary.

He looked at her so differently now. Not at all the way he'd gazed at her the night before. Gone was the passion, the intense heat that had burned between them. Her heart ached at the thought of all she was about to lose and all that they might have shared.

Maybe Lamar was right. She could have loved Jack Beaumont. Perhaps she already did. But Jack had made his feelings crystal clear regarding her criminal past. *She* might be able to love *him*, but he could never love her.

"I'm glad I found you," Maddie said, trying to keep her voice from trembling. "I have something for you."

"What is it?" Jack asked.

Maddie pulled the envelope from her pocket and held it out. "It's your return ticket to San Francisco. And a check to cover your daily rate. You'll have to send me a bill for your expenses."

"You're firing me?"

She nodded her head. "I don't need you anymore." Maddie swallowed hard and a warm flush crept up her cheeks. Why were the words coming out so wrong? "I—I mean, I don't need you to guard the judge. The funeral is Friday morning."

Jack seemed surprised by her announcement. "Three days. That's soon."

"I spoke with Sheriff Dilby. He's ready to concede that our plan to catch Lamar's murderer isn't working. It's best to put Lamar to rest. It's time," Maddie said.

"I'll stay until the funeral," Jack said. "You might need me." He paused and gave her a chagrined smile. It seemed she wasn't the only one thinking about their encounter the night before.

"No. That's not necessary. You should go home. There's nothing left to do here."

"But I want to stay. I've grown rather attached to the judge over the past week."

Maddie didn't know what else to say. She had to find some way to make him leave. Until he did, the judge would have to stay dead. Everyone would be forced to continue this charade until *she* called an end to it. "About last night," she began.

"I wanted to talk to you about that," Jack replied, stepping closer.

Maddie shifted nervously, clutching the airline ticket in her hand. "If you think—I mean, if you expect that there's going to be…something between us, then I have to tell you that there won't. What happened last night was a mistake. It won't happen again."

"A mistake," Jack repeated.

"Yes. A big mistake. We should have never—well, we just shouldn't have. So if that's the reason you're staying, then you don't have to."

He stared at her with a frozen expression, his blue eyes slowly turning hard as stone. She wanted to sink to her knees and scream, to pull her hair in utter frustration. She didn't want him to leave! She wanted him to yank her into his arms and pick up where they'd left off the night before, right here and now on the garden path. Instead, she summoned her resolve.

"You did your job well," she said. "I asked for your loyalty and your discretion and you gave me both. But the job is done. And it's time for you to go." She pushed the ticket at him until he was forced to take it. "Your flight is tomorrow morning."

"Maddie, I—"

She shook her head. "Don't. Let's just leave it at that." She held out her hand, then tried to keep it from trembling. "Thank you, Mr. Beaumont. For everything."

Her took her fingers in his and stared down at their joined hands. His fingertips softly stroked the inside of her wrist, and after a long moment, she pulled her hand away. "I better go. Calpurnia will have dinner for you whenever you're ready. If I don't see you tomorrow morning, have a pleasant trip back to San Francisco."

She spun on her heel and hurried toward the house, toward the safe and secure environment that had sheltered her for over fifteen years. But she couldn't feel safe at Felicity. Not until Jack Beaumont had gone far away, leaving her alone to repair her fractured heart in solitude.

JACK RODE ALONG the Gulf Coast Highway with the top down on the rental car, enjoying the blazing heat of midday and the bright sunshine. His bags were packed and tossed in the back seat.

He'd left Felicity early that morning, knowing that Maddie would still be asleep. They'd said their goodbyes the day before, so he'd slipped out while the house was still silent, afraid that if he saw Maddie again he wouldn't be able to leave. The airport was only a ninety-minute drive from Fells Crossing, and he was nearly three hours early for his flight when he approached the exit on the interstate.

But at the last minute, he veered back into the center lane and continued on, through New Orleans, across the water to the other side of Lake Ponchartrain. Before he knew it, he was in Mississippi. By then he had decided on another plan.

A quick phone call to Pensacola Naval Air Station gave him a new destination. Though it was almost a four-hour drive, the time passed quickly as he sped through a changing landscape, past the beaches of Gulfport and Biloxi, across Mobile Bay and into Pensacola.

Another call to an old buddy from the teams got him onto the base and ranked a ride over to the airfield, where he watched the jets come and go. An hour later, he was lounging in the ops center when Lieutenant Jefferson Beaumont brought his F-18 Hornet back to home plate.

Jack watched from the doorway as his brother strode toward him, his flight suit unzipped, helmet tucked under his arm. He looked much bigger than Jack remembered him, and older. Though they'd written once or twice a year, talked on the phone a few times, it had been twelve long years since they'd last seen each other in person. Jack stepped out onto the tarmac. "Hey, Sparky! Was that a trash hauler I saw you flying?"

Pushing down his sunglasses, Jeff squinted, then stopped dead in his tracks. "Geez Louise. Jack? You're the last person I expected to see. What the hell are you doing here?"

Jack shrugged, staring at the kid who had turned into a man. Jefferson Beaumont. He hadn't seen Jeff since his baby brother's graduation from Annapolis, just a few short weeks before everything had fallen apart in the Beaumont family and Jack had gone into self-imposed exile. "I don't know. I was in the area and I thought I'd drop by."

"In the area? Where?"

"I'm working a job near Baton Rouge."

Jeff shoved his helmet at Jack, hitting him square in the gut. "That's not exactly nearby. That's a half day's drive. What are you doing over there?"

"Personal security."

"You're a professional goon?" Jeff joked. "And here I was thinking you might have been working as a hit man in some exotic locale. Or tracking down arms dealers with the CIA."

"I'm a bodyguard. Are you going to bust my chops or are you going to buy your big brother a beer?"

Jeff grabbed Jack around the neck, then yanked him into a bear hug. "God, it's good to see you. Let's go over to the O club. I've got a powerful thirst."

Jack gave his brother a playful shove and feigned a few punches. "Will they let me in? I'm not an officer anymore. I'm just a lowly civilian."

"As far as I'm concerned, you're still Lieutenant Jackson Beaumont. Just don't tell them you were a frogman. We sky jocks like to think we're the toughest guys in the navy."

Jack glanced at his brother, frowning. "How did you know?"

"That you were on the teams? Navy's a small world, Jack. And you and your team had quite a reputation. Mom and Dad got all your postcards. And your letters from the Gulf."

Shoving his hands in his jeans pockets, Jack nodded. "Postcards were an easy way to avoid visits."

"I have to say Dad was kind of surprised that you resigned your commission," Jeff said, pointing to a jeep parked next to the ops center. "And he would have been pleased as punch to know you were on the teams."

They climbed inside and Jeff punched the accelerator, driving the same way he flew, with controlled abandon. "I was ready to get out," Jack shouted over the sound of the engine. "At least after I blew out my knee and they booted me off the teams."

"Why didn't you ever tell Mom and Pop you were a SEAL?"

"I thought Mom would worry less if she thought I was some intel drone. We were into some pretty nasty stuff over in the Middle East. And then there's always the comparisons to Pop. Besides, training takes almost five years. I wasn't sure whether I was going to wash out or not."

Jeff swung the jeep out onto the street, the tires squealing. "SEAL training is tough. He wouldn't have blamed you if you'd washed out. He was a SEAL. He knew how tough it was."

"Beaumonts don't wash out," Jack said, a sarcastic edge to his voice. "We're gung-ho guys, truth and honor types. God and country." Jack leaned back in the seat and raked his hand through his windblown hair. "Jim Beaumont left some pretty big swim fins to fill. And then after...well, you know."

"Cynthia? Hell, Jack, you can say her name."

"Why? So I can remember how she tore our family apart? You forget, Mom and Dad sided with Jay. They didn't believe me. They believed her."

The jeep pulled up to the officer's club and skidded to a stop. Jeff turned to him, a serious expression on his angular features. "You always were the rebel in the family, big brother. What were they supposed to think? I don't remember a day going by when you didn't push the edge of the envelope."

Jack nodded, knowing his brother spoke the truth. He had been a real pain in the ass, always jumping into everything with his hair on fire and his fangs out. He'd approached Maddie Parmentier in the same way, treating her like some hill to be conquered, some LZ to be secured.

They hopped out of the jeep and strolled into the officer's club. The place was nearly empty. They snagged a few stools at the bar and ordered a pair of beers. "So you've been good?" Jack asked, settling onto the bar stool.

Jeff shrugged. "Yeah. And you?"

"Good," Jack said. A long silence settled between them.

"You know Jay got married again," Jeff offered. "It's been almost three years now. They already have a couple of kids. A little boy and baby girl. I got home for Christmas last year."

"No kidding," Jack said. "Two kids. That's great. Hell, I guess I have been out of touch."

"He married a research scientist, of all things. Her name's Susannah. She's really sweet, the perfect match for Jay. He's running the boat yard for Dad. Designing sailboats. What about you? Any women in your life?"

Jack paused, fixing his attention on his beer bottle. "There is one," he admitted. "In fact, I'm working for her. Or I *was* working for her. Madeline Parmentier."

"You're guarding her?"

"I guarded her dead husband." Noticing Jeff's confusion, Jack added, "He was dead before I got the job."

Jeff laughed out loud. "Well, that's a relief. It wouldn't do to be chasing after a woman whose husband was alive."

Jack sighed. "Yeah, but I think she might have helped get him that way. Dead, I mean."

"You're in love with a murderer?"

Taking a long swig of his beer, Jack considered the question. He set the bottle down. "Who said I was in love?"

"No one. But that hangdog expression of yours is a big clue. You got it bad, big brother."

Jack idly scraped at the beer label with his thumbnail. "Yeah, I guess I do. I don't want to believe she killed him, but all the evidence points in that direction."

"What does your gut tell you?"

A soft oath burst from his lips. "That Maddie Parmentier isn't a murderer. That she loved Lamar Parmentier. And maybe I'm just trying to heap all this suspicion on her because I want to believe she's not worth having."

"Makes a pretty compelling reason to stay away from her."

"When I was in the navy, I didn't think about settling down and getting married. I saw what Mom went through while Dad was gone and I knew I couldn't make it work, not if I wanted to be a SEAL. But now that I'm out, I've been thinking about it a lot. If I were going to settle down, I'd want a woman like Maddie."

"So make it happen," Jeff said. "You're a creative guy. You've been in tougher spots. If you want her, then go after her."

"But I'm not sure she's the one," Jack replied, rubbing his forehead in an attempt to brush aside the confusion. "How am I supposed to know for sure?"

"You're asking me? I don't know. Call Jay and ask him. He's the one who got married."

"My best buddy from the teams just got married, too. I'm starting to think there's no way to avoid it.

Kincaid didn't seem the type to settle down at all. But even he fell fast and hard—for a woman he'd been employed to protect." For a single guy, working at S. J. Spade could be downright dangerous.

"So is that why you came here? To ask me for advice on your love life?"

Jack stared at the colorful rows of bottles behind the bar for a long moment. "Naw. I've been thinking about the family a lot. Thinking about trying to patch things up. I really made a mess of it, didn't I?"

"Believe me, Jack, there's nothing to patch up. Mom and Dad would love to see you. Jay is happy. And I think they stopped believing Cynthia a long time ago."

Cynthia. Her name still brought a flash of anger and a flood of regret. She'd used him, playing him against Jay, against his whole family. She had been a master manipulator. Jack took another long swallow of his beer. "Maybe I'll take a trip back to Baltimore. For some reason, I feel like I have to straighten things out."

He'd never been one to worry about the future. But ever since he'd arrived at Felicity, he'd found himself longing for a place to call home, a place to put down some roots and enjoy life. Part of it was probably age. But most of it was Maddie.

He wanted to wake up with her in his arms and fall asleep with her by his side. He wanted to watch her cook and listen to her chatter on about vegetables and sauces and the evils of lard. With her, every day was fresh and new and full of surprises. He barely knew her, yet he already knew he couldn't live without her.

Jack closed his eyes and bit back a curse. Even after all the suspicions and doubts, he still couldn't bring himself to believe that Maddie wasn't worth loving.

And he did love her. He couldn't deny that fact any longer.

With a soft groan, Jack pushed back from the bar and stood up. "I have to go," he muttered, slapping Jeff on the shoulder. "Little brother, you take care."

Jeff slid off his bar stool. "You're going? But you just got here."

"I know. But I've got some things to straighten out. Next time you talk to Mom and Dad, tell them I'm going to be making a trip home real soon. I've got a lady I want them to meet."

"Maddie the murderer?" Jeff asked.

Jack chuckled and strode toward the door. "She's not a murderer, Lieutenant Beaumont. She's the woman I love!"

RUSH HOUR TRAFFIC in New Orleans put Jack behind schedule. When he drove up the front drive to Felicity, it was nearly dinnertime. He didn't bother to grab his bags, but decided instead to get right down to business. There were a few things he intended to discuss with Maddie Parmentier, things he'd been going over in his mind for the past six hours.

He wasn't quite sure how he was going to tell her. Jack Beaumont had never uttered those life-changing words. So he had practiced in the car. And once or twice on the front steps before walking inside. "Maddie, I love you," he murmured. "I love you, Maddie, and I want us to be together."

Taking a deep breath, Jack grabbed the doorknob and flung the door open. "Maddie?" His voice echoed through the silent house. "Maddie?"

Hurried footsteps sounded in the hallway above him, and a few moments later, she appeared at the top of the stairs. She gazed down at him for a long moment. "What are you doing back here? What do you want?"

He tried to speak, but the sight of her had stolen his breath away. She wore another one of those pretty dresses of hers, the fabric loose and flowing and clinging to her limbs. She was barefoot again, and her dark, tousled hair curled around her lovely face.

When he had left Felicity, she had been Madeline Parmentier, a woman he had shared a few intimate encounters with. But now, as he stared up at her, she was Maddie, the woman he loved. The woman he wanted to spend his life with.

And Jack wanted that life to begin now. He took a step forward, but she held out her hand to stop him. "Maddie, we have to talk."

Her fist clenched and she shook her head. "I thought you'd left."

"I had. But I'm back."

She looked away, fighting back her emotions. Then she met his gaze, her eyes filled with determination. "We don't have anything to say to each other," she said in a cool voice. "Just go. Go back to San Francisco. Go home, Jack."

She turned and walked away, but Jack was not going to let that be the end of their conversation. He'd driven like a bat out of hell to get back here, and it wasn't going to end like this! Taking the stairs two at a time, he caught up to her outside the upstairs parlor.

Jack grabbed her shoulders and turned her to face him. Though her expression remained composed, he could see the anxiety in her green eyes. Myriad emotions flickered there—anger, regret, frustration, sadness. He leaned toward her, hoping to kiss away everything that stood between them. But she pulled back and shook her head.

"Please don't do this," she said, evading his lips.

"I have to," Jack murmured, his gaze fixed on her mouth. "God, Maddie, I don't want to love you. But I can't stop myself."

"Don't say that," she pleaded, her voice raw.

He bent closer to kiss her, but she pulled her hand back as if to slap him. Instead, he turned and touched his lips to her open palm. A tiny moan escaped her throat as his mouth drifted down along her wrist, his teeth biting and nipping. "I need you, Maddie."

"No," she said.

He kissed her elbow, then moved up her arm. "Yes," he countered.

"I don't want you," she said, the words catching in her throat.

"I don't care." He traced a line over her shoulder, along her collarbone to her neck. And by the time he reached her mouth, she had abandoned all pretense of resistance. Her breath came in quick pants and her eyes were closed, her head tipped back.

A rush of desire overwhelmed him the instant their mouths met. Frantic with need, he cupped her face in his hands and molded her lips to his. He was like a man parched with thirst, desperate to drink in the taste of her until he was completely sated.

Maddie, sweet Maddie. She'd bewitched him from the moment they'd met. And now there was nothing he could do but give himself over to the spell she'd woven around him. He didn't care about anything but this—his mouth on hers, his hands skimming over her body.

"Tell me you don't care," he murmured against her swollen lips. "Tell me you can just walk away. There's something happening here, Maddie, and ignoring it isn't going to make it stop."

She shook her head and wove her fingers through his hair, pulling him back down to kiss her again. As he did, her hands gripped his shirt, holding on so tight that he wondered if she'd ever let him go again.

"We can forget the past, Maddie," he said, raining gentle kisses over her flushed face.

As if a cloud had scudded in front of the sun, the light of desire drained slowly from her. She stiffened, then pulled back, and when she opened her eyes the haze of passion had cleared and her features had gone cold.

"I can't," she said, shaking her head.

She hurried into the parlor, as if it might provide an escape. But he followed her tenaciously, determined to make her see his way. "What do you mean, you can't?"

"Jack, I'm asking you to leave. Please."

"I won't," Jack said. "We belong together."

She pressed the heels of her hands to her temples and sent him a tormented look. "Are you listening to yourself?" she cried. "We've barely known each other a week."

"Who cares? When it happens, it happens."

"We're strangers. We've shared a few intimate moments, but nothing more. Nothing to build a future on."

"I'm not going to let your past come between us," he said, a hard set to his jaw. He stepped back and crossed his arms over his chest.

Maddie paced in front of him, growing more agitated with each step. "My past? What do you know about my past?"

"I don't want to know!" he said. "That's the point. We're starting right here and now. What happened before doesn't matter."

"It's who I am," she said. "And it matters to me."

"Why are you being so stubborn?" Jack demanded. "Do you realize what it took to get me back here? You're not exactly what I imagined when I thought about falling in love."

A flash of pain crossed her face and he instantly regretted his words. But he couldn't take them back. He could only watch her rising indignation, the high color in her cheeks, the bright flash of anger in her eyes.

"So, there it is," she said, her voice tinged with bitterness. "I knew that would come up sooner or later."

"That," Jack said caustically. "All right, if you want to get it all out, let's do it. Let's talk about 'that.' In fact, let's just call 'that' what it really is."

She tipped her chin up. "Go ahead, say it."

"Murder," Jack said. "There, are you happy?"

Maddie's eyes went wide and she gasped. For a moment, her knees wobbled and he thought she might fall right over. She couldn't have reacted more strongly if he'd knocked the wind out of her. "What?"

"You heard me."

"I—I can't believe you said that."

"Someone had to."

This time he didn't see the slap coming. Nor could he stop it with a few well-placed kisses. Her hand cracked across his cheek with such force that it caused stars to appear before his eyes. He'd been decked by the best of them, but nothing came close to the power of Maddie Parmentier's anger—and her right cross.

"Get out!" she cried.

Geez, why was she so angry? He knew what she was hiding and he'd just told her that he didn't care! She should be kissing him and weeping in relief. Instead, she stood toe-to-toe with him, not showing any sign of backing down. "Hell, no. I'm not leaving," he replied.

She stamped her foot. "Get out of this house! Or—or I'll have Truett toss you out."

Jack grinned and rubbed his face, then flexed his stinging jaw. "No way."

A sputter of anger was all she could manage before she whirled and stalked toward the door. "Then—then I'll get out," she cried from the doorway. The parlor door slammed behind her, rattling the pictures on the wall and making Jack wince.

"Well, now," he muttered. "If that's the way things are going to go between us, I'm looking forward to the marriage proposal."

With a deep sigh, Jack flopped down into a wing chair and rubbed his forehead. He sat there for a long time, their conversation running through his mind. He couldn't fight the notion that he was missing something, a piece of the puzzle that made up Maddie Parmentier. He hadn't expected such a fierce reaction from her. In truth, he'd thought she would be relieved that it was out in the open.

And he'd also expected an explanation. He knew Maddie couldn't have murdered Lamar. She wasn't capable of taking another life. But she could know how he'd died. She could be covering up for someone else. Or maybe she'd caused his death by way of an accident.

Jack frowned. He'd come back for the truth and he wasn't any closer than he had been sitting in the officers' club at Pensacola. He glanced over at the coffin. "Dead men tell no tales," he murmured.

Bracing his elbows on his knees, he leaned forward. "I'm kind of sorry we never had a chance to meet," Jack said, staring at the coffin. "I know how much

Maddie cared about you. And though I'm not sure what went on in those last days, I'm willing to believe that she would never deliberately hurt you. I don't think it's in her nature."

He chuckled softly. "But then, I guess you knew her a little better than I did. Or at least I hope you did. Hell, I'm not even sure you two were married. But if you were…"

Jack slowly pushed himself out of the chair and crossed the room. "If you were, I guess I'm asking your permission. Not that I believe in ghosts, but I wouldn't want you haunting me because I horned in on your wife. I'm in love with her. I don't know how it happened, but…" He smiled. "Well, I guess I don't have to explain that to you. You probably know what she's like. After all, you married her—maybe."

He ran his hand over the smooth wood of the coffin's lid. His thumb brushed against something, and he looked down to find it was the lock. He reached for the edge of the lid, then pulled his hand away. So he was curious. What guy wouldn't be when offered the opportunity to size up the competition? Granted, a dead guy wasn't much of a threat. But Maddie had loved Lamar Parmentier and Jack loved Maddie.

He reached out again, his hand trembling slightly. "Geez, Beaumont, get a grip. It's not like he's going to bolt up from the dead and grab you by the throat. Come Friday, everyone's going to be staring at him. You're just getting an early look."

Drawing a calming breath, Jack closed his eyes and slowly pulled, but the coffin wouldn't open. With teeth clenched, he pulled a pocket knife from his jeans and jimmied the lock. It popped open with barely any effort. He'd get a look at this paragon of virtue, this man that Maddie had either loved or murdered.

The lid creaked in protest as he pushed it up, and he winced. Man, he had faced some pretty rough sights in the SEALs, but the thought of gazing down on a week-old corpse gave him the heebies.

He cursed himself. "All right," he muttered. "Give me a three count, Beaumont. Three...two...one." He opened his eyes, blinked twice, pinched his eyes shut and then opened them again. It didn't help. He still couldn't believe what he saw.

"Oh, hell." He dropped the lid, then furrowed his hands through his hair.

The coffin was empty.

# 7

THE DOOR TO MADDIE'S bedroom crashed open. Fully dressed, she sat up in bed and scrubbed at her watery eyes, her heart leaping into her throat. When she had made her escape from the parlor fifteen minutes before, she'd hoped that Jack would just get in his car and leave.

"Where is it?" His voice filled the room, as intimidating as his figure in the doorway. In the low light of the setting sun she couldn't see his features. She didn't need to see his face to know that he was angry.

"Go away," she cried, throwing an embroidered pillow in his direction.

"What did you do with him, Maddie?"

"With who?"

"Lamar! He didn't just get up and crawl out of that coffin!"

Maddie's heart did a back flip. She scrambled off the huge tester bed and smoothed her wrinkled skirt, only to grab it up in her clenched fists. "You—you opened Lamar's coffin?"

"What did you do with him? Did you hide the body? Or maybe there never was a body in there. Maybe you disposed of poor Lamar long ago. Tossed him in the river or buried him in the rose garden."

She wiped her sweaty palms on her skirt, then laced her fingers together behind her back. "No, we were going to do that to you," she murmured. "Luis was right. You would have made good compost."

Jack ignored her and stepped inside the room, closing the door behind him. "No wonder there was never an autopsy."

Maddie walked over to the open French doors and stared out into the growing darkness, her nerves jangling, her heart thudding. The scent of flowers drifted in on the evening breeze and she took a steadying breath. "There was no autopsy because there never was a body," she said, her back to Jack.

"Yeah, right. Now you're going to tell me that Lamar simply decomposed more quickly than your average corpse. I've heard all the stories about what an extraordinary man he was, but I don't think even *he* could have managed that."

Maddie turned and shook her head, surprised by the thread of jealousy she detected in Jack's voice. "I think it's time I ex—"

Her words were drowned out by the sound of glass and wood shattering near her ear. A spray of splinters and shards of glass stung her bare shoulder. Maddie cried out, and an instant later, she found herself on the floor, Jack lying on top of her. She shook her head, trying to rid herself of the ringing in her ears. Birds had flown into the open French doors before, but they'd never broken a window.

"That must have been a big bird," she said, stunned and confused, listening for the flapping of wings.

"Don't move," Jack warned.

He lay on top of her for a long time, long enough for her to realize that she couldn't breathe. "Will you get off me?" she said, wriggling beneath him. "It's just a bird!"

"Dammit, Maddie, hold still!"

She shoved against his shoulders. "If this is som
new method of seduction, I don't like it! My arm i
falling asleep and there's something digging int
my—"

Jack clapped his hand over her mouth. "Quiet!"

She pried his fingers off her mouth. "I will not be—

"That was a gunshot," Jack said, his face just inche
from hers, his breath warm on her lips. "Stay her
Keep quiet. I'm going after the shooter."

Maddie frowned, grabbing him by the front of hi
shirt and yanking him nearer. "Someone tried to shoo
me? With a gun?"

Jack scrambled to his feet, and when she tried t
rise, he pushed her back to the carpet. "By the looks o
it, they damn near succeeded."

"Wait!" Maddie cried, grabbing at his ankle. "You
can't go out there. What if you get shot?"

Jack sidled over to the door, staying close to the wal
as he peered out into the shadows of the gallery. The
he sent her a crooked grin. "You *do* care."

She growled in frustration and pounded her fists o
the plush carpet. "Of course I care. I don't want you
bleeding all over the gallery. We just had it painted
last spring!"

By now he had moved outside. He glanced over his
shoulder. "Honey, I've been shot at by the best o
them. And I haven't been hit yet."

With that, he was gone. Maddie closed her eyes and
said a silent prayer. Why did he have to be a hero?
Why couldn't he just crawl under the bed with her
and hide until someone called the sheriff?

All right, maybe she didn't have to worry. It was
probably just an accident, a hunter's stray shot. Or
maybe Emile was cleaning the judge's antique pistols

and had loaded one just for fun and... Why would anyone want to kill her?

"He's a bodyguard," Maddie whispered. "This is what he gets paid for—standing in the way of bullets. He'll be fine. He'll be fine." But as she waited for what seemed like endless hours, she slowly became aware of how much Jack Beaumont meant to her. Over the past week, she had tried to deny her feelings for him, but with a rather large bang, they had become crystal clear. If anything happened to Jack, she would never forgive herself.

"I love him," she said, the words hitting her like a ton of bricks. Maddie threw her arms over her eyes. "Oh, God," she moaned. "What am I going to do?"

The bedroom door flew open and Maddie heard a flurry of footsteps come toward her. "Madeline! Are you all right? Have you been hurt? Don't move. Truett will call the sheriff. And the doctor."

She pulled her arms away from her eyes and looked up at Lamar's distressed expression. His face was flushed, as if he'd run all the way from the river to the house, and his white hair stood on end. Calpurnia hovered behind him, wringing her hands in her apron. "Just lie still, missy."

Maddie pushed up on her elbow, then sat. "Don't worry about me," she said, brushing herself off. "I'm fine. But Jack—he went after the guy with the gun." Unbidden tears burned in her eyes and she groaned, brushing at them angrily. "What if he gets shot? I mean, I finally find a guy I can love and now he's going to be dead. I told you both this would happen. I'm not supposed to have a happily ever after. I don't deserve it."

Lamar squatted down and patted her shoulder, then turned to Calpurnia. "Except for a few superficial

scratches and a nasty case of self-pity, I think ou
Madeline will survive."

A few moments later, Jack stalked back into the
room and immediately came over to Maddie's side
He bent down on one knee, and she grabbed him and
hugged him tight. "You're not dead," she said, run
ning her fingers over his face. "Oh, I'm so glad."

"Are you sure you're all right?" he asked. Hi
hands skimmed over her body, looking for injuries
His fingers stilled on her left shoulder. "You're bleed
ing."

She craned her neck and shrugged. "It's nothing
Just a little sliver of glass. What about you?"

Jack pulled her into his arms and pressed his lips to
the top of her head. "I'm fine. Damn, that must have
been a big caliber gun. You can still smell the powde
in here. Did someone call the sheriff?" He glanced
around the room, which was slowly filling—first with
Emile, then Luis and then Truett—before his gaze
came to rest on Lamar. "Who are you?"

Maddie winced as she carefully extricated herse'
from the circle of his arms. She stood up and Jack
straightened beside her. "Jack Beaumont, may I intro
duce Lamar Parmentier."

Lamar stepped forward and held out his hand. "]
can't thank you enough for protecting Madeline. I
you hadn't been with her she could have been seri
ously injured."

Jack's astonished gaze jumped from the judge to
Maddie and back again as he shook Lamar's hand. I
he was going to yell at her, he'd probably do it now
Maddie waited for the eruption of anger, but Jack re
mained silent.

"It's Lamar," she repeated. "He's not really dead."

"I can see that," Jack replied.

"That's why the coffin was empty. When someone tried to kill Lamar, he and Sheriff Dilby decided that we should pretend that he had died. And then the sheriff started the rumor around town that Lamar hadn't died, just to stir things up a bit."

Jack rubbed his forehead as if trying to absorb all this new information. "Let me see if I understand," he said. "This was all a ruse to draw the killer out. And I was part of that ruse. So you didn't lie about that."

Maddie nodded. At that moment, Sheriff Dilby came lumbering into the room. He took a few minutes to check Maddie over, then questioned her thoroughly about what had happened. Jack added his version of the story, before the sheriff began to examine the room for evidence.

He circled the perimeter, looking at the broken window and at the far wall near Maddie's dresser. Maddie watched him as Calpurnia tended to the tiny cut on her shoulder. Dilby pulled out his reading glasses and slipped them on, then squinted at a spot on the wall. "Here it is," he said, taking a pocket knife from his jacket. A few seconds later he crossed back to the group and held out his hand. "Does that look like a minié ball to you, Lamar?"

Lamar picked the slug up and examined it. He smiled grimly. "That's a minié ball, all right, Dudley."

The two of them shared a long look, then Dilby turned to Jack. "You're the bodyguard here. I'm goin' to need your help, son. I want you to guard Madeline until we figure out who did this. I'll post deputies on the gallery. You keep her on the second floor—away from the windows. Don't let her out of your sight." Dilby grabbed his gun and held it out to Jack. "Here, take this."

"I don't need it, Sheriff."

"Oh, yeah, I forgot. You Navy SEALs can paralyze a man with a writin' pencil. Problem is, I'm plumb outta pencils at the moment."

"I've got a gun," Jack said. "It's down in the car."

"Well, a lot of good it did you down there. Take the gun, son."

Jack nodded mutely and grabbed the weapon, then stole another glance at Lamar. Maddie tried to read his features, but his expression was emotionless. His initial reaction to her revelation had faded and he'd become a silent observer, taking in everything and everyone around him without comment.

Dilby clapped the judge on the shoulder. "Lamar, I'm afraid you're going to have to get dead again. I don't have enough manpower to put a guard on you, as well. If they tried to take a shot at Maddie, they'll jump at another chance to shoot you."

With that, the sheriff and Lamar left the room. Emile and Luis trailed after them, followed by Truett. But Calpurnia refused to let go of Maddie's arm. "Are you sure you're all right, missy?"

Maddie smiled and squeezed her hand. "I'm fine. Why don't you and Truett go fix yourself a nice soothing cup of tea? I have a lot to explain to Jack."

When they were finally alone, Maddie sat down on the edge of the bed and folded her hands on her lap. Jack prowled the room, drawing the heavy drapes over the French doors and making his own examination of the bullet hole in the wall. It was apparent he was on edge, and Maddie searched for the proper words to explain the situation. But there was no good way to couch the truth in feeble excuses.

"Jack, I—"

"I don't like this, Maddie," he interrupted, bending down to look at the broken glass on the Oriental carpet. He used the muzzle of the sheriff's pistol to pick through the shards. "They're not telling us everything. I mean, what the hell was that with the bullet? A minié ball? Didn't that seem a little odd to you? I don't know many criminals who use a Civil War-era gun to commit murder. They know something."

"If—if Sheriff Dilby knows who tried to kill Lamar, why hasn't he arrested someone?"

Jack straightened and walked to the bed. "I don't know. But thanks to his shoddy detective work, whoever tried to kill Lamar is now after you." He sat down beside her, but kept a safe distance between them. Bracing his elbows on his knees, he examined the sheriff's pistol, as aloof and preoccupied as Maddie had ever seen him. She started to take his hand, but he drew away.

"I—I know this comes as a big surprise," Maddie began. "And I owe you an explanation. But I want you to—"

"Just tell me one thing," Jack said, turning to her, his gaze suddenly intense, his eyes searching her face.

She wanted to reach out and smooth the worry from his forehead, to wipe away the lines of tension that bracketed his mouth. Even more, she wanted to lose herself in his arms, in his kisses. The charade was finally over. She didn't have to lie to him anymore. But he seemed so restless, distracted by what had happened. "What do you want me to tell you?"

"Do you love him?"

The question took her by complete surprise, and she answered without even thinking. "Lamar?" Maddie smiled. "Of course I love him. I did all this to protect him."

Jack's lips pressed into a hard line. He was silent for a long time. "You're not a widow anymore."

Realization slowly dawned and Maddie laughed. "No, I'm not a widow," she said. "I never was." She paused, biting at her lower lip. What must be going through his head! she mused. As far as she was concerned, it was time for this whole charade to end and for her relationship with Jack to finally begin. "And I'm not a wife, either."

JACK STARED AT HER in bewilderment. He wasn't sure what to make of her startling statement. At first he assumed he'd misunderstood. But what other meaning could be attached to her words? "I don't get it. You aren't a wife?"

Maddie gave him a guilty little shrug. "I'm not married to Lamar. I never was."

"But you're involved?"

"No," she said, shaking her head slowly. "Not that, either. Lamar and I have a very...special friendship."

"Special, how?" Jack wasn't sure he wanted to hear her answer, but he couldn't keep from asking. He didn't want to hear how much she loved him, how they were meant for each other. How there had never been another man for her.

"He's like the father I never had. And I guess I'm the daughter he never had. My parents weren't around when I was younger, and Lamar, he—"

Jack held out his hand to stop her from speaking. All of this was just a little too much to take in. In less than thirty minutes, Maddie had gone from a murdering, scheming widow to a happily married wife to a never-been-married daughter. "If you weren't married to Lamar, why did you pretend to be his wife?"

"To protect him," she said, completely unaware of how illogical that sounded to Jack. "To provide an excuse to keep his coffin in the parlor. Lamar has no living relatives, except of course for you, his third cousin, twice removed."

"Second cousin," Jack corrected.

"Lamar and Sheriff Dilby thought it would be best. We couldn't have the sheriff coming out here once or twice a day to keep the *staff* informed of the investigation, and we needed him to come out here so he could communicate with Lamar."

"If Lamar wasn't in the coffin, where was he?"

"Sometimes he stayed here in the house on the third floor, in Truett and Calpurnia's apartment. And sometimes he stayed in the old boathouse on the river. There's a passageway that leads from the parlor down to the cellars and then out to the gazebo by the river. The tunnel was built during the war."

"He was in the parlor, talking to you that night I came in? And down by the river, too?"

She nodded. "We talked every day."

"But why pose as his wife?"

"There were all sorts of questions about the funeral," Maddie explained. "The will, what would happen to the house, whether the staff would stay or go. It just seemed easier to keep things running smoothly until Lamar rose from the dead...so to speak. A wife could continue to run the household without drawing any suspicion. That is, until Eulalie Rose Peavy opened her mouth."

Jack's temper suddenly flared and he cursed out loud. "But what about *your* safety? Did they even consider that they might be putting you at risk? Geez, Maddie, someone tried to kill you! You came this close to getting a bullet in the—" He bit back his words, then took a calming breath. "You could have been killed."

A frown worried her forehead and she sighed.

"That's what I don't understand. Why would someone try to kill me? Dilby believes that one of the men Lamar sent to prison is behind this. Some guy who got out a few weeks before Lamar tasted the poison in his brandy. The sheriff just needs time to figure out where the guy is."

"Have they considered any other suspects? What about a relative?"

"I told you, Lamar doesn't have any relatives."

"Not that you know of. Maybe not that he knows of, either. As I see it, the only reason for killing you would be to open up a challenge to Lamar's will."

Maddie gave him a quizzical look. "You mean Lamar might have a briar-patch child?"

"I mean an illegitimate child."

"That *is* a briar-patch child," Maddie said. "But I don't think that's possible. Lamar married Miss Sarah when he was barely twenty, and back then people didn't—well, you know, not before they were married. Not that I think there's anything wrong with doing...it. Before you're married. That's just a matter of personal—"

"Maddie!"

"Well, he never, *ever* would have cheated on her."

"Something isn't right," Jack muttered, pacing back and forth in front of her. "I think Lamar and Sheriff Dilby know more about this than they're telling you."

A soft knock sounded on the door. Maddie rose to open it, but Jack warned her away. He motioned her back toward the bed, then moved to the door and slowly opened it.

Calpurnia stood on the other side, a huge tray in her hands. She hurried forward and placed the food on an antique piecrust table between two wing chairs. After a quick rearrangement of the chairs, she glanced over at Jack and then at Maddie. "I thought you two might want some dinner. Cold fried chicken," she said. "Fried in canola oil. With fresh warm biscuits and potato salad and iced tea."

Maddie crossed the room and peeked under the linen towels laid over the meal. "Thank you," she said before kissing Calpurnia's cheek.

The older woman clucked her tongue, then sent Jack a warning scowl. "You watch out for our girl," she said. "If anythin' happens to Maddie, I'll person'ly take it outta your sorry hide." With that, the cook gave him a disdainful sniff, turned on her heel and strode from the bedroom.

"Are you hungry?" Maddie asked.

Jack shook his head. He was too worried to eat. Worried about what had happened here in this very room. Worried about what was happening outside in the darkness surrounding Felicity. He didn't have much faith in Sheriff Dilby or the "deputies" that he planned to summon. No doubt the boys from the barbershop would help out.

"I'm not hungry, either," Maddie said, turning to watch him from the other side of the room. "I'm really just exhausted."

"Why don't you get some sleep?" he said, momentarily distracted by her gaze. "I'll ask Calpurnia to take the food away for now. Her wide green eyes skimmed over his face, and a tiny smile curled the corners of her lips.

"I—I suppose I could do that," she said, moving toward him. "Are you going to stay? Here in the room, with me?"

"I'm not leaving you alone, Maddie. For the first time in a week, I'm going to do the job I'm qualified to do."

Maddie walked around him to the bed. If he didn't know better, he'd swear she was flirting with him, enticing him. The way she brushed against his shoulder as she passed, the way she coyly watched him from beneath dark lashes, the way she stretched her arms above her head as she stood next to the high tester bed, working the kinks out of her neck. It all seemed incredibly seductive.

A slow knot of desire tightened in his gut, and he fought the temptation to grab her from behind and toss her onto the bed. There was nothing standing between them now—not Lamar, not the silly scheme to protect the judge, or Jack's ridiculous suspicions. Nothing…except the man outside in the dark who'd tried to kill her.

Jack berated himself inwardly. He was not going to let his lust get in the way of protecting the woman he loved. There would be plenty of time for passion after Maddie was safe. No matter how hard she tried to lure him into her arms, he'd simply have to ignore her.

"I need to change," she murmured, glancing at him over her shoulder.

Jack swallowed hard. This was going to be more difficult than he'd thought. "All right," he replied in a tight voice. He walked over to the French doors and pulled the heavy drapes open a bit, peering into the dusky night. "I'll keep my back turned. Go ahead."

He focused his attention outside, but a reflection in one of the unbroken glass panes caught his eye. He should have dropped the drapes, but he couldn't. Instead, he crushed the thick brocade in his fist as he watched a wavy image of Maddie. Mesmerized, he could barely breathe as she unbuttoned the back of the dress she wore. It fell down around her ankles and she stepped out of it, wearing only panties and a lacy scrap of a bra.

Jack sucked in a sharp breath and closed his eyes. But he couldn't resist another look. She had tossed her underwear aside and was standing with her back to him, naked. As she reached over to grab her nightgown from the bed, he caught a tempting glimpse of her breasts. His gaze drifted lower, to the gentle curve of her hip, her perfect backside, her slender legs.

He felt himself grow hard. How the hell was he supposed to keep his mind on the job at hand when Maddie was just a few feet away—and naked? It was almost a relief when she slipped the silky nightgown over her head and pulled on her robe.

"All right," she said.

He didn't want to turn around. His arousal would be plainly evident to anyone but the half-blind Emile, and Mattie would realize he'd been observing her in secret. Jack decided to continue his survey of the growing twilight, willing his desire to subside.

"Jack?"

"Hmm?" The image of her still lingered in his head. God, she was beautiful. He'd never wanted a woman as much as he wanted Maddie. He knew if he stepped over to the bed and took her in his arms they would make love, right here, right now. She would be so sweet and soft and seductive, responsive to his every—

Jack cleared his throat, then turned around to find her staring at him inquisitively. "So?" he said.

"So," she repeated.

"You're going to sleep now?"

"Yes," Maddie said. "I'm going to try." She pulled back the covers of the bed and crawled beneath the crisply ironed sheet, then methodically smoothed it over her legs. When she'd settled back into the downy pillows, she sighed. "Where are you going to sleep?" she asked.

Jack shrugged. "I'm not going to sleep," he mumbled. "But I'll be close by."

"You could come over here and lie down with me," she suggested, patting the mattress beside her. "We could...kiss."

Grinding his teeth, he ran his fingers through his hair. The offer was oh so tempting. "Maddie, I've got a job to do and I intend to do it. Kissing you and lying with you in that bed would seriously distract me."

"That's what I was hoping for," she said. "A distraction. This whole thing has me a little...nervous. I'm scared."

The last was said in such a tiny voice that Jack couldn't help but give in to her request. Hell, he'd been shot at a hundred times and it spooked him every time. But Maddie had no experience with life-and-death circumstances. She had never faced that kind of fear, the sudden brush with mortality.

In a few long strides, he crossed the room and sat down on the bed, gathering her into his arms. "You don't have to be scared, sweetheart. I'm right here with you. I'll keep you safe. I promise."

Maddie nuzzled his chest and sighed. "I'm glad you know the truth," she murmured. "About Lamar. I didn't like lying to you. And I didn't like you thinking badly of me."

He looked down at her, tipping her chin up and brushing his mouth over hers. "Maddie, you did a brave and honorable thing for a person you loved. You could have trusted me with the truth, but you were only doing what you thought best. I'm ashamed that I ever believed you capable of a crime."

He saw a momentary flash of regret in her eyes and she stiffened slightly in his arms, but then she pulled him nearer and kissed him full on the mouth. For an instant, he allowed himself to get lost in the taste of her, the feel of her lips against his. He longed to explore her body, to learn every curve, every intimate detail; to tug off the robe and nightgown and look upon her body.

With one final attempt at self-control, Jack pulled away. He traced a line along her moist lips with a fingertip. Then he gently guided her down between the sheets and pulled the top one up to her chin. Dropping a gentle kiss on each of her eyes, he smiled. "Go to sleep, Maddie."

She curled up beside him, her arm wrapped around his waist. Jack placed the gun on the bedside table, then closed his eyes. He tried to push aside tantalizing images of her, above him, beneath him, around him, but each time he tried to focus on something mundane, she'd dance back into his brain again, taunting him with the promise of what they'd soon share.

"When you're safe," Jack murmured. As he held her close, he realized that he'd do anything to protect her. He'd give his life to save hers. And in that moment of clarity, he knew that he truly loved her.

THE DISTANT SOUND of the morning birds told Jack the sun was up. He hadn't slept a wink the entire night, tensing at every unfamiliar sound, assessing it before eliminating it as harmless.

He glanced down at Maddie. She had tossed aside the bedclothes and was now curled up beside him, her robe twisted and her nightgown bunched to reveal the pretty length of her legs. Her dark hair fanned across the pillow, and he reached out and twisted a strand around his finger.

She looked so peaceful and innocent. That's what he loved about Maddie—her innocence. Though she was probably as experienced as any woman her age, there was something about her that was almost childlike. Was it her trust? Or her unwavering loyalty to Lamar? Or was it the way she looked at him, as if she were experiencing desire for the very first time?

Jack smiled to himself and brushed the strand of hair behind her ear. There were so many things he didn't know about Maddie. A few days ago that had frustrated him. Now he found it intriguing. They'd take their time together and learn about each other, discover each other as they went along. As soon as she was safe, he reminded himself. Then their life could start.

Jack heard footsteps on the gallery and held his breath. But they passed, and he wondered which of Sheriff Dilby's deputies was on watch this morning. Taking care not to wake Maddie, Jack disentangled himself from her, then quietly slid off the bed.

He walked over to the French doors and pushed back the drapes. Sunlight flooded the room and he squinted against the brilliant glare. Then he pulled the shattered door open and poked his head outside. Dilby stood at the railing, just a few feet to the right.

"See anything last night?" Jack asked.

Dilby kept his eyes on the rose garden, his back to Jack. "One of my deputies found some footprints in the garden. Now that the sun's up we can look for more clues."

Jack grasped the doorknob with a white-knuckled hand. He wanted to shout at the man, to insist he call in more competent help. Maddie was still in danger and the sheriff was leaving it up to amateurs to collect evidence. Jack schooled his temper. His priority was protecting Maddie. If he had to fly her back to San Francisco and lock her inside his apartment in order to keep her safe, then that's what he'd do, and Dilby's investigation be damned.

"I'm going to go down to the kitchen and get some coffee," Jack said. "Maddie's still asleep. Stay right here until I get back."

The sheriff glanced over his shoulder and nodded, then went back to his perusal of the garden. Jack closed the door behind him and walked to the bed. He bent down and kissed Maddie on the cheek, but she didn't stir.

As he checked the room for security once more, Jack stopped at the vanity in the corner. He picked up one of Maddie's perfume bottles and held it to his nose, drawing in a deep breath. Closing his eyes, he remembered that night on the riverbank when he'd kissed her. And the night in the library when he'd nearly made love to her on the leather sofa. She had been wearing this scent.

He picked through the other things scattered over the shiny mahogany surface—lipsticks, a brush and two combs, a tube of perfumed hand lotion. As he turned away, he noticed her purse tucked behind a cookbook written in French. Jack reached for the purse, then pulled his hand back. He didn't need to know any more. She would tell him everything in time.

But he couldn't help but be curious. He was in love with the woman and he wasn't even sure of her last name. Hell, he didn't even know where she lived or what her birthdate was. Just a quick peek at her driver's license wouldn't be such a terrible invasion of her privacy, would it?

Jack looked over at the bed, then snatched up the purse and withdrew her wallet. He found her license, then turned it toward the thin sliver of light that came through the crack in the drapes.

"Delaney," he repeated, letting the name linger on his lips. "Madeline Delaney." He liked the sound of that. Maddie Delaney. Maddie Delaney Beaumont. Maddie Beaumont.

According to the Louisiana Division of Motor Vehicles, she lived in New Orleans on Magazine Street. He frowned. Magazine Street was where he'd followed the woman into the restaurant. Delaney's. The restaurant on Magazine Street, the place he thought he'd seen Maddie enter had been called Delaney's.

Jack slipped her wallet back inside the purse, then returned the purse to its proper place. Suddenly all the pieces fell into place. The judge and his devotion to social causes. He'd taken people out of their lives of petty crime and given them jobs. Calpurnia, Truett— every employee at Felicity had a past. And he'd probably given Maddie a chance at a better life. That's why she'd been so set on protecting Lamar, because she owed him.

Jack's first impulse was to call the agency, to have Mark run a background check on Maddie Delaney. But then he realized that he didn't care. Whatever Maddie had done was in the past. If a man like Lamar Parmentier could forgive and forget, then Jack certainly could.

He knew enough now. She was an accomplished chef and he'd be willing to bet money she owned the restaurant on Magazine Street. That's why he'd seen her at the French Market and again near the restaurant. He walked back toward the bed and looked down at her for a long, lingering moment.

"Maddie Delaney," he murmured. "It's a pleasure to meet you." Jack reached down and caressed her cheek with his fingertips. She stirred at his touch and her eyes fluttered, then opened. She looked up at him and gave him a smile.

"Are you awake?" he asked.

"Umm. It's so dark in here. What time is it?"

"I don't know. Maybe around seven."

Maddie wove her fingers together and stretched her arms above her head. "I slept so well," she murmured, a hesitant smile touching her lips

Jack brushed the hair out of her eyes and tweaked her nose. "I'm glad."

She pushed herself up on her elbow and tucked her hair behind her ear. "And I'm famished. Is that tray still here? I could have one of those biscuits and some tea."

"Tell you what," Jack said. "Why don't you just lie back down and I'll go make you a decent breakfast. A navy breakfast. I'll put my sauté skills to work."

She glanced over at the French doors, then back at him, worry marring her sleepy features.

"It's all right," Jack said. "Dilby is right outside. You'll be safe until I get back."

She lay down again, snuggling into the pillows. "A navy breakfast in bed," she said. "That would be nice. And maybe after, we—we should talk about what happened last night."

Jack chuckled, then bent down and gave her a quick kiss. "Stay put, Maddie. I'll be back in a few minutes."

As he strode down the stairs, Jack found himself whistling a cheery little tune. Life was just about per-

fect. The sun was shining, the birds were singing and
the woman he loved was waiting for him in bed. As
far as he was concerned, the only thing they needed to
talk about was their future together.

# 8

MADDIE STRETCHED beneath the covers and sighed. What a perfectly perfect morning! For the first time in over a week, she'd had a good night's sleep. No more troubled dreams about her past, or fears for Lamar's safety. Now that Jack was on the case, they were sure to find out who had caused all this trouble.

She closed her eyes and nestled her face into the pillow. And now that Jack knew the truth, there would be nothing to stand between them. A sliver of doubt shot through her. Well, he didn't know the whole truth, but at least he didn't believe she was a murderess anymore.

And the rest she had all worked out. Maddie was honest enough to know that if they did make love, it would probably be a short-lived affair. Jack had his life in San Francisco. And she had hers in New Orleans. In a sense, there was just enough standing between them to keep any worries about the future at bay.

They could share a few passionate nights together and then part without regret. Besides, she really didn't want a permanent relationship, did she? Casual sex allowed her to keep a few of her secrets. Committed sex meant that she'd have to tell him everything—every sordid detail about her past.

Maddie buried her face deeper in the pillow. Why was she so ashamed of what she'd been? There were

hundreds of celebrities who jumped at the opportunity to publicize the mistakes they'd made in their
lives—the addictions, the failed relationships, bizarre
sexual proclivities, and even a few crimes worse than
hers. She should be proud of what she'd managed to
accomplish! And Maddie was.

People did change. But inside, she still felt like that
street kid, only this time she wasn't snitching wallets
from drunken tourists, she was snitching bits and
pieces of happiness from an unsuspecting man.

But Jack was getting something from the deal, too,
wasn't he? She couldn't really consider him a victim.
And as long as they kept their relationship light and
casual, she didn't owe him a recitation of her life's
story. Now that she knew the judge had sealed her records, she would never have to worry about her past
again.

With a lazy smile, Maddie turned over and drew
her arm up over her eyes. Everything would be just
fine. She sighed, then tried to fall back asleep, but
thoughts of Jack kept running through her mind.
When he returned she would convince him to forget
breakfast in bed and move on to more interesting activities. What had Eulalie called it? Conjugal calisthenics? Since she and Jack weren't married, they'd be
forced to enjoy calisthenics of the carnal type.

A flash of light penetrated her eyelids and she knew
the drapes had been thrown open to the early morning
sun. Maddie smiled contentedly. "That was quick,"
she murmured. "You can't have breakfast for me already, can you?"

"Lazy little trollop!"

Maddie's breath caught in her throat at the sound of
a vaguely familiar voice. She bolted up in bed and

rubbed her eyes, squinting into the glare of sunlight that poured through the window. "Who are you?"

The silhouette slowly stepped forward, and an instant later Maddie's gaze focused on Eulalie Rose Peavy. "Miss Peavy! What are you doing here?"

The older woman was dressed, as always, in her distinctive style. This morning she wore chiffon, bright turquoise blue, with a satin sash and a high, ruffled neck. A huge hat with ostrich feathers covered her gray hair, the feathers swaying wildly with every movement of her head. Maddie's fashion inventory stopped when her gaze fell on the huge rifle that Eulalie held beneath one arm. Though she knew better than to question the woman's choice of accessories, Maddie was quite certain that a gun was not a typical part of Eulalie's fashion world.

"That's right," Eulalie said. "If you know what's good for you, Jezebel, you'll do exactly what I say."

Fear snaked through Maddie's consciousness. "Miss Peavy, please. Put the gun down. You have no quarrel with me."

"I don't?" Eulalie hefted the rifle higher, pointing the barrel in Maddie's direction. Maddie's heart leaped to her throat. Where was Sheriff Dilby? And where was Jack? Why had no one stopped Eulalie from entering the house?

It didn't take an instant for Maddie to realize that Eulalie had been the one who had shot at her the night before. The gun she held looked like an antique, but Maddie knew that it was capable of sending a minié ball right through her body in the same way it had shattered the plaster of the wall.

A sudden thought brought a wave of nausea washing over Maddie. Could Eulalie have shot both Dilby and Jack before she made her way to Maddie's bed-

room? No, Maddie would have heard the gunfire. A
maelstrom of anxiety assailed her. She had to keep
calm! If she could engage Eulalie in conversation, then
perhaps Jack would come back in time to save her.

"No one's going to come to save you," Eulalie said,
as if she'd read Maddie's thoughts.

"What did you do? Where is Sheriff Dilby?"

"Lying out there with a big old knot on his noggin."

Maddie was afraid to mention Jack. Maybe Eulalie
wasn't aware that he was in the house. *Keep her talking,*
Maddie told herself. "Lamar wouldn't like you pointing that gun at me," she said.

"What do you know about Lamar? He was *my*
friend! He cared about *me!*"

"I'm sure he did. He still does," Maddie said. If she
told Eulalie the truth, maybe she'd put the gun down.
But then logic told her that if Eulalie was the one who
had tried to shoot her, then she had also put the poison in Lamar's brandy. "You should know that—"

"Hush up!" Eulalie snarled, hoisting the rifle up
against her shoulder. "I don't want to hear you talkin'
about my Lamar!"

"Your Lamar?"

"He loved *me.* From the time we were children, we
were promised to each other. Then he went off to that
fancy college and met Miss Sarah. Well, I bided my
time, waitin' for my chance. And when she passed on,
I knew Lamar would fall in love with me."

"Sarah died a long time ago," Maddie said.

"I—I got tired of waitin'," Eulalie said, her voice
suddenly weary.

"So you poisoned Lamar?"

Suddenly the gun seemed to grow heavy in Eulalie's hands. Her arms began to shake and her chin
trembled. "I just wanted to make him sleepy. Then I

was going to slip into his bed and allow him to compromise my honor. He would have *had* to marry me then."

"Eulalie, if you put the gun down, I'll take you to Lamar."

The woman shook her head, the feathers dancing in the air. "No. It's too late."

"It's not too late. He's—"

At that instant, everything seemed to grind into slow motion. The bedroom door opened and Maddie turned to look. Eulalie swung the muzzle of the rifle and aimed at the door. Maddie screamed at Jack, then scrambled off the bed, the sheets twisting around her legs. The gun exploded, filling the room with the acrid scent of spent gunpowder, and Maddie closed her eyes, unable to watch.

And then, as quickly as it had begun, it was over. Jack stood in the doorway, a breakfast tray in his hands, staring at Eulalie as plaster dust from above the door drifted down on his dark hair. Maddie choked out another warning, but he turned and smiled at her.

"It's a muzzle load," he said. "She only had one shot and she missed."

Maddie felt the blood rush to her head and she thought she might faint. She sank back down into the pillows, pulling in deep drafts of air, and watched as Jack dropped the tray on a table, crossed the room in three long strides and grabbed the rifle from Eulalie's hands.

Eulalie slowly collapsed to her knees, weeping uncontrollably, a wailing lump of blue chiffon and ostrich feathers. She'd barely begun to beg for forgiveness when Sheriff Dilby appeared from the gallery, nursing a huge bump on his forehead.

A minute later, when Lamar and Truett ran in from the hallway, Eulalie was inconsolable. She looked up long enough to see Lamar, then burst into another round of sobs and incoherent babbling. When he realized it would be useless to try and interrogate her, Dilby turned her over to three of his deputies. They tried to haul her up off the floor, but she refused to stand. Finally, Lamar spoke to her in soft words and she agreed to leave.

Maddie turned to Jack, only to see fury raging in his eyes. "Jack? Are you all right?"

"You knew," he said, taking a step toward Lamar and Dilby. "You both knew it was Eulalie."

Dilby glanced at Lamar nervously, and Lamar nodded. "We suspected," he said.

"All along? From the start?"

"That's why we didn't make a big commotion with the investigation," Dilby replied. "Lamar wanted to keep it quiet. Eulalie's always been a few sandwiches short of a picnic. She's an old family friend. She didn't belong in jail."

"She tried to kill Lamar!" Jack cried. "And she damn near killed Maddie. Twice!"

"She didn't mean to kill Lamar," Maddie offered. "She just wanted to get him into bed."

Dilby blinked in surprise. "Now there's an interestin' motive. Listen, Beaumont, we didn't think she'd come around and start shootin'. We've been lookin' for her since last night."

"How the hell did she get past you?" Jack asked, his voice nearly a growl.

The sheriff rubbed his forehead again and scowled. "She surprised me from behind. Tapped me on the shoulder, and when I turned—bam—she cracked me on the head with the butt of that old gun. Came out of the parlor, she did."

Lamar cursed softly. "Eulalie knows about the passage from the river. We used to play in the tunnel as children."

Jack's jaw tensed, a muscle twitching just beneath his ear. "I want you to lock her up," he said, his voice deceptively calm. "And throw away the key." He glanced around the room "Now get out of here. All of you. Leave us alone."

No one put up an argument. Maddie wasn't even sure she wanted to stay, considering Jack's mood. But when she started toward the door, Jack grabbed her hand and slipped his fingers through hers, pulling her to his side. "You're staying with me," he murmured.

The door closed behind Dilby and Lamar. The room grew silent. Smoke from the rifle still hung in the air, turning the bright morning sun into a soft, dreamy haze. "I—I guess it's all over," she said, glancing up at Jack.

Jack's jaw tensed. "Not by a long shot," he murmured.

His arm snaked out and he pulled her close, molding her body to his. Then, with a soft curse, he brought his mouth down on hers. The urgency of his kiss took her by surprise. It was as if he needed to prove to himself that they both were alive and well.

"I never should have left you alone," he said, his words frantic against her lips.

"I'm all right," Maddie replied, her hands skimming his face, wiping away the tension and the guilt. "I am. It's all over now."

But Jack was right. It wasn't over. There was still something standing between them and he was determined to bring it crashing down. His kiss slowly became less about relief and more about unbridled passion. He ravished her mouth, biting and nipping and teasing at her tongue. She wanted to stop him, to assure him that she was all right, but Maddie found herself swept away by his uncontrolled desire.

She had never known a man who could turn a simple kiss into such a powerful act of passion. His mouth worked its magic on her senses and there was no way to resist. Capitulation was her only option. Oh, what Jack Beaumont could do with his lips. Such sweet torment, such dizzying delight.

"You have too many clothes on," he murmured, his fingers clutching at the tie of her silk robe.

Maddie chuckled. "Then take some of them off," she challenged.

Jack looked down at her and his expression softened. All the guilt and self-recrimination slowly faded. With a crooked grin, he unknotted the belt and brushed the silk robe off her shoulders. It slipped to the floor, puddling around her feet.

"Oops," he said.

She was exposed to his touch, and he trailed his tongue along her jawline, over her collarbone, lingering for a long moment on the sensitive skin just above her breasts. Maddie shivered, arching her head back and closing her eyes.

She was already lost. Even if she wanted to stop him, she couldn't. She had relinquished all capacity to refuse him anything but the most intimate caress. He slipped his fingers beneath the thin straps of her nightgown and slid them over her shoulders.

When his lips covered a pebbled nipple, Maddie sucked in a sharp breath, raking her fingers through his thick hair. Then he moved on in a gentle exploration of her body with his mouth and his tongue. Inch by inch he tugged her nightgown down until it hung from her hips.

"Don't you dare ask me to stop, Maddie," he murmured against her hip. "I don't think I can."

She stepped back and looked down at him, then smiled. Her hands skimmed the nightgown off her hips. The silk slipped sinuously down her legs and then it was gone. "I don't want you to stop," she said. "We're just getting started."

With a low growl he stood up and captured her face in his hands. Her fingers worked at the buttons of his shirt, until, frantic to do away with every barrier between them, he tore at them himself. His jeans came next and he tossed his wallet on the bed. Maddie watched, taking great delight in his fast-forward striptease. But when he'd peeled down to just his boxers, she stopped him.

She had expected to be nervous. Maddie didn't have much experience with men, especially the naked, in-the-bedroom, fully aroused type of man. But Jack was different. With him, she felt safe. He'd protected her; he'd saved her life. And she knew that he would never do anything to hurt her.

"God, you're irresistible," he murmured, reaching out to run a finger along the curve of her breast. "Like a dream come true."

A secret thrill shot through her, and Maddie sighed. For the first time in her life, she felt beautiful and sexy, like a real woman. She'd never learned all the little tricks for charming a man, the coy smiles, the sensual movements, the suggestive words. Before this, it had only been playacting. But that didn't matter now. She didn't need tricks. Jack wanted her for who she was. And she wanted him.

Maddie placed her palm on his smooth chest. Beneath her fingertips, she felt his heart beating, strongly and evenly. Sunshine poured through the window, gilding the muscles of his torso and the sinew of his arms. This was pure decadence, to make love in the light of day, the doors and drapes to the gallery tossed open to the morning breeze.

She hooked her thumbs under the waistband of his boxers and slowly pushed them down to his feet. When she straightened, their gazes locked. "Make love to me, Jack Beaumont," she said as she stepped into his embrace, her naked body pressed along the length of his. "And don't stop until I say so."

Jack laughed, then scooped her up in his arms and tossed her onto the bed. They rolled and twisted and taunted each other, alternating between passion and play, drawing out the inevitable until neither one of them could bear to wait any longer.

Teasing hands slowly turned frantic; incoherent words mingled with soft gasps. And a slow heat began to build between them. Maddie reached for him, took him in her hands and gently stroked his burning desire. He moaned softly, then rolled her on top of him, her knees straddling his hips.

They locked gazes, and for a moment, neither one of them could breathe or move. It was all so perfect, so intense, she didn't want it to end. Yet when Jack reached out and cupped her sweat-slicked breast in his palm, there was nothing she could do to stop a headlong rush into ecstasy.

She sheathed him in the condom he retrieved from his wallet. Then he pulled her beneath him, settling his weight between her hips. And with a low moan, he slipped inside her and began to move—first slowly, then with greater urgency, driving away all rational thought, all emotional control.

"Oh, Jack," she breathed, stunned by the power of their coupling. Pure sensation raced through her bloodstream, pooling at the core of her being, electrifying every nerve. She murmured his name over and over again, more frantic as the knot of desire tightened within her.

Suddenly, an overwhelming shudder rushed through her and she tensed. She felt herself swell around him. And then she shattered, crying out with the numbing mixture of pleasure and pain. He joined her just moments later, reaching his climax as she descended from hers.

When they were both completely spent, he slipped to her side and wrapped his arm around her waist. For a long time, they didn't say anything, just lying there, exhausted, their bodies shiny with sweat.

"Wow," he murmured.

"Umm," she replied.

"I can't move. You've paralyzed me. I'll never be the same."

Maddie turned and nuzzled his cheek. "I'm famished," she said.

He rolled his eyes, feigning exasperation. "Why is it you're always hungry when there's never any food close at hand?"

"I love to eat," she said, nipping at his jaw. "I live to eat."

He kissed the tip of her nose. "You like food more than sex?"

"Well, I did...until a few minutes ago." Maddie rolled to her other side and looked at the table near the door. "I need more energy. What about your breakfast?"

"It's just cereal, juice and coffee," he said. "And

some toast and fruit. Calpurnia was in the kitchen and wouldn't let me use the stove."

Maddie rolled onto her back and pulled the sheet up to her chin. "Feed me," she murmured. "Or I won't let you make love to me again."

Jack laughed as he crawled off the bed and retrieved the breakfast tray. Maddie took in the view of his long, muscular legs, his narrow waist and wide shoulders. And that gorgeous backside. She smiled to herself, glad that she hadn't volunteered to fetch the tray herself.

He placed the meal between them, then sat at the end of the bed, cross-legged, the end of the tangled sheet pulled across his lap. Maddie looked over his culinary choices. "Did you cook anything on this tray?" she teased.

"Toast," he said. "I cooked the toast."

She snatched up a piece of the stone cold bread and bit into it. "Umm, very good. Toast has been perplexing the great chefs for a long time. Toast and soufflés. I'm glad to see that you've mastered it so quickly."

"Yes, I've worked with all the great chefs," Jack boasted, stretching out and clasping his hands behind his head. Her gaze fixed on the muscles that bunched and rippled across his chest and abdomen. "Chef Boyardee. Chef salad. Chef—rolet?"

Maddie giggled at his silly joke and fed him a piece of cold toast with jam. She reached out to wipe a bit of the sticky strawberry from his mouth, then sucked it off the end of her finger.

"Marry me," Jack said, between chews.

Maddie slowly removed her finger from her mouth, staring at him in astonishment. "What did you say?"

"You heard me. I want you to marry me."

She dropped the toast on a plate and snatched up a

napkin. "But—but we've only know each other a week."

"Ten days," he corrected. Jack leaned forward, drawing himself up on his knees. "Maddie, when I was in the SEALs, I got used to acting on instinct, making split-second decisions with my life hanging in the balance. I learned to go with my gut, and my gut tells me that we belong together...forever."

"Maybe it's just indigestion," she said. "From the warm orange juice."

He took her hand and laced his fingers through hers. "Maddie, I'm serious. I want you to be my wife. I've almost lost you twice in the past twenty-four hours. I'm not going to risk losing you again."

"But, Jack, we hardly know each—"

He pressed his finger to her lips and pulled the breakfast tray from between them. Then he quickly covered her mouth with his, pulling her up to her knees. His kiss was impossibly persuasive, sending a tingle of warmth from her fingertips down to her toes, feeding a new hunger that surged through her. Oh, she could imagine waking up with this man for the rest of her life. And falling asleep in his arms every night.

Jack slid his palms over her backside and yanked her up against his growing hardness. "It will be incredible," he murmured. "You and me. And kids. Lots of kids."

He didn't wait for an answer—Maddie knew he assumed her reply would be yes. She couldn't tell him that he was wrong. Instead, she let him make love to her again and again, in so many different ways, letting the day slip away in blissful oblivion. And each time he brought her to her peak, she died a little inside.

When he finally fell asleep in her arms, she stared

up at the ceiling, waiting for darkness to fall. And fo
the light to go out of her life.

SHE DIDN'T WANT TO LEAVE him. Maddie could have
spent the rest of her life in his arms, listening to his sof
breathing as he slept, curling into the safe circle of his
arms. Never had she felt so secure, so completely
loved.

Somewhere in the house, a clock chimed, and she
counted the hour. It was 10:00 p.m. If she left now, she
could be back in New Orleans, back home, by mid
night. She fought down a wave of self-indulgent tears
then chided herself for losing the grip on her emo
tions.

The entire week had been an emotional rolle
coaster, with tears popping into her eyes at the
slightest provocation. Maddie Delaney never cried
yet she couldn't seem to stop herself now. Lying with
her head on Jack's chest, she listened to his heartbeat
strong and slow, and gathered the tattered shreds of
her resolve.

Maddie turned and pressed her lips against his coo
skin. Everything had been under control. She'd con
vinced herself that she and Jack would give in to their
passions, enjoy a few days at Felicity and then go their
separate ways. It had been such a simple plan.

After all, she knew he wasn't the type to settle down
and she'd been glad. Maddie Delaney had never se
much store in happily ever afters. Love was nice for
other people, but not for her. After all, how could a
person trust a feeling that was supposed to last for
ever, a feeling that was supposed to transcend all trou
ble? Nothing lasted forever. Nothing was that resil
ient.

Yes, everything had been under control—until he

asked her to marry him! She drew in a deep breath and slowly squirmed her way out from his embrace. But as soon as she broke contact with his touch, she felt lost. Cold and empty inside, she fought the urge to crawl back in beside him.

"I can do this," she murmured. "I have to do this."

She stood next to the bed and looked down at him, trying to memorize every feature of his face as the warmth of his body slowly faded from her skin. His hair was mussed into boyish waves, and he slept with his arm thrown over his eyes, like a loose-limbed child. The sheet tangled around his narrow waist, leaving his long, muscular legs as bare as his chest.

Maddie's fingers clenched as she remembered touching him, exploring his body and drawing her palms over smooth skin and hard muscle. He was like no man she'd ever met. He had loved her, with his heart and his mind and his body. But she couldn't accept his love any more than she could accept his proposal of marriage.

Marriage! Maddie had never even considered that option, never suspected that he might ask. When she thought about the future with Jack, marriage had never entered the picture. After all she'd been through in her childhood, she'd always assumed she would never find a man to spend her life with—or she'd never be asked. The concept was so totally foreign to her that she couldn't even imagine it—the wedding, the little house with the picket fence...the children.

She took a step back from the bed, closing her eyes with a determined oath. It had all been so good, so perfect...until he'd asked her that awful question. With a stifled sob, Maddie turned and searched the dark room for something to wear. She could barely see, but she managed to find the clothes she had taken

off the night before. Lord, she'd spent the last twenty
four hours inside this room! No wonder she was suc
an emotional wreck.

Hurriedly, Maddie slipped into her underwea
then pulled the dress over her head. A quick search o
the floor beneath the bed turned up her espadrilles
Her purse was the last item she needed before she lef
the room. But when she reached out to open the door
she stopped.

Could she really do this? Could she just walk awa
without saying goodbye? Goodbye would require ex
planations, and Maddie wasn't sure she even kne
why she felt compelled to leave. All she knew was tha
the longer she stayed, the greater her fear grew.

Fear of what? Was she afraid that she'd come to de
pend on him, only to have him leave? She'd dealt wit
loss before, first of her father, then her mother. Peopl
were always abandoning her. Perhaps she was afrai
she'd lose her independence. Since she was a kid
she'd called her own shots. She didn't want to be re
sponsible for another person's happiness.

Maddie sighed. If she stood here long enough, sh
was certain she could come up with a litany of excuse
for walking out. But she didn't need a list! Just lik
Jack, she'd lived her life by instinct, knowing when t
hold and when to fold. It was definitely time to tos
this hand, before she got in over her head and lost to
much.

She took one last look at the man who slept s
soundly in her bed. Then, as if drawn by an invisibl
force, she crossed back to him. Silently, she ben
nearer and placed a gentle kiss on his parted lips
"Goodbye, Jack," she murmured. "If ever there was
man I could love, you were the one."

An errant tear tumbled from her eye and plopped

on his beard-roughened cheek. Maddie reached out with a hesitant hand to brush it away, but then clenched her fingers into a fist and drew her hand to her chest. She rubbed at the ache in her heart and it slowly disappeared beneath a veil of numbness.

"You'll always be the one." With that, she turned and hurried to the door. This time she didn't hesitate. Maddie knew if she didn't leave now, she'd never leave.

The hallway was dark and silent. The soft carpet disguised her footfalls, and as she dashed down the stairs, she forced her thoughts away from Jack and to the future.

New menus for the restaurant...the way he caressed her face when he kissed her...an expansion plan for Delaney's dining room...the intense blue of his eyes...the price of salmon...the incredible sensation of surrender when he entered her.

"Stop it," Maddie muttered. "Stop torturing yourself!"

She shoved open the door to the kitchen, then stopped dead in her tracks. A quick escape without notice was what she'd been hoping for. But Lamar, Truett, Calpurnia and the rest of the staff at Felicity sat gathered around the table, a huge bowl of popcorn in the middle and the remains of a late-night poker game scattered about.

"Hi," she murmured. "What are you all doing up?"

"Lamar just got back from the hospital," Calpurnia said. "He and Dilby took Eulalie over for observation. And what are you doing up?"

"I—I'm leaving," she said, attempting to keep her tone light. "I've been away from the restaurant for so long and Anne has been watering my herb garden and

writing out the schedule and ordering the fish and
just can't stay away any longer."

"What about Jack?" Lamar asked, munching on a
handful of popcorn.

"Oh, Jack," she said. "Well, he'll be leaving in the
morning, I suppose. He has to get back to San Francisco."

Lamar gave her the same look he'd used when she
had misbehaved as a teen. The look that said he expected better from her. "Madeline? What's going on? I
thought you said you were in love with him."

Maddie twisted her fingers together and shifted un-
easily. "He wants to marry me."

Everyone at the table gasped in unison, then
jumped up and congratulated her, clapping each other
on the shoulders, caught up in their own delight.
Maddie held out her hand. "No, no," she cried. "I'm
not going to marry Jack Beaumont."

Truett stared at her as if she'd lost her mind. The
rest of the group followed suit. "Why not?" Truett
asked.

"You don't understand! He asked *me* to marry *him*!"

Calpurnia chuckled. "And what's wrong with that?
I 'spect the man's in love with you."

"No! I mean, yes, he does love me. But that doesn't
make any difference. I still can't marry him."

"Madeline, what are you afraid of?" Lamar asked.

Maddie ran her fingers through her tangled hair.
"I—I don't know. I just know that I *am* afraid. And
when I think about marriage, I get this queasy feeling
in my stomach. Like I ate too many of Calpurnia's
hush puppies. I just want to…throw up."

Calpurnia snorted. "Are you ever goin' to stop with
your rant on lard?"

Lamar sent the cook a warning look. "Everyone's a

little scared when it comes to marriage," he said. "It's a mighty big step. But you'd make a good wife, Madeline. And a fine mother."

"That's so," Calpurnia added with a nod. "I'll stand by those words."

Maddie considered the notion for a long moment, then winced. "He—he wants a family. He wants children. But I don't know anything about families. I don't know how to be a mother or how to make a child love me."

"You don't have to make a child love you," Calpurnia said. "That comes naturally."

"No, it doesn't," Maddie replied, shaking her head vehemently. "I tried to love my mother, but I'm not sure that I ever did. And she certainly didn't love me. Maybe there's something in my genes. A—a defect. That's it! I'm defective."

Lamar pushed himself away from the table and stepped to her side, then wrapped his arm around her shoulder. "You're scared," he said. "Not defective. You're looking for any reason you can find to protect yourself from getting hurt. But sometimes, Madeline, you have to toss aside your fears and go for it."

"Go for it," Luis said.

"Yeah," Jim Bob cried. "Just go for it."

Emile gave her a thumbs-up.

But no amount of encouragement would change her mind. She slipped out of Lamar's reach, then grabbed her keys and hurried to the back door. "I'm sorry," she said. "I wish I was braver, but I'm not."

The judge crossed his arms over his chest. "Stop underestimating yourself, Madeline."

She forced a smile. "When Jack gets up, he's probably going to be a little angry. Don't tell him where I am."

"He'll know to find you at the restaurant," Lamar said.

"No. He doesn't know about the restaurant. He doesn't really know anything about me, not about my past—or my present. He doesn't even know my real name. Please, promise you won't tell him."

They all stared at her with indifferent expressions.

"Please," she pleaded. "You're my friends. My—my family. I need you to do this one thing for me."

They looked at each other, silently agreeing on a response, then Lamar nodded. "All right. We'll do as you ask."

Maddie sighed in relief. "Good," she said. "Thank you."

She gave them all a little goodbye wave, then walked out the back door to her car. Once she got to New Orleans, she'd feel better. She'd slide back into her normal routine and she'd be so busy, she'd forget all about Jack Beaumont. Before long, she'd be able to get through an hour without his image drifting through her mind. And then a day, and after that hopefully weeks at a time.

She would overcome Jack Beaumont the same way she had overcome her childhood, her years on the streets and her criminal past. With sheer will and unwavering determination.

# 9

"YOU LOOK LIKE HELL."

Jack rubbed his aching head, then squinted up into the early morning sunshine. Even his sunglasses didn't provide protection from the pounding in his temples. "I feel like hell," he muttered. With his foot, he shoved a chair out from the other side of the table and nodded toward it. "Sit down, little brother. Order yourself a cup of coffee and one of these..." He pointed to the puffy confection on his plate, covered with powdered sugar. "I can't remember what they're called. But they're damn good for a hangover."

"Beignets," Jeff said, sliding into one of the chairs that littered the sidewalk outside the Café du Monde. He ordered a cup of coffee, then leaned back in his chair and studied Jack. "When was the last time you slept?"

Jack shrugged. "I'm not sure. I've been enjoying the *bon temps* here in the Big Easy. There's no time to sleep. I'm having too much fun *rouler*ing or *laissez*ing or whatever they want you to do down here."

"You want to tell me what happened?" Jeff asked.

Jack took a sip of the strong, black, chickory coffee, then grimaced when it burned his tongue. "Why do you think anything happened?"

"I get a call from you at 1:00 a.m. last night, asking me to meet you in New Orleans asap. I scramble to get

a few days emergency leave and then I arrive to find
you here, hungover and crying in your coffee."

"What were you expecting?" Jack said.

Jeff shook his head. "I was kinda thinking you
might have decided to get married. And maybe you
wanted me to be your best man."

Jack's sharp laugh caused the other early morning
patrons of the café to glance his way. "Now there's op-
timism. Foolish though it may be."

"You want to tell me what happened?" Jeff asked.

Jack wagged a finger in his brother's direction.
"Women. That's what happened. I was going along,
minding my own business, getting the job done and—
wham! She hits me like a sidewinder and my whole
life just blows up in front of me."

"Don't you think you're being a little dramatic?"

Jack leaned over the table, bracing himself with his
elbows and affecting a thick Southern accent. "I'm
pilin' on the agony, little brother. I got myself a powerful case of the can't hardlies. And the only cure for
that is bourbon, straight up." He chuckled. "See? I've
already been here too long. I'm starting to talk like
them."

Jeff took a sip of his coffee, then added a liberal dose
of cream and sugar. "So, can I assume that you and…"

"Maddie," Jack said. "Madeline Delaney."

"You and Madeline Delaney had some kind of
fight?"

"I wish," Jack said. "We spent one incredible night
together. And then she snuck out while I was asleep,
and took off."

"Sounds like one of your old tricks," Jeff said with a
chuckle.

"Well, if I had known how much it hurt, I would

ave at least said goodbye to a few of those women.
Maybe even stayed for breakfast a time or two."

"Hey, you're probably better off without her. The
oman might have offed her husband. You don't
eed to be associating with the criminal element."

"She didn't." At Jeff's curious look, Jack could only
nake his head. "Don't ask. It's too complicated to ex-
lain."

"I've got time. A two-day leave."

"The condensed version? She didn't murder the
uy. He's still alive. And she was never married to
im in the first place."

"So everything's cool with this woman you love,
othing's standing in your way, and you've spent
ow many nights drowning your sorrows in bourbon?
eez Louise, Jack. Go after her."

"Don't think I haven't been tempted!" His enthusi-
sm faded fast and he braced his throbbing head with
ne heel of his hand, rubbing at a knot of tension in his
orehead. "Hell, she doesn't want me. She made that
erfectly clear when she snuck out of bed in the dead
f night."

Reaching over the table, Jeff clapped Jack on the
noulder. "Let me impart a bit of my considerable
fe's wisdom regarding women. What they *do* and
ow they *feel* often have no logical connection at all.
hat's Jefferson Beaumont's seventh maxim of the fe-
nale sex. I've made it my mission to figure out
romen, and I have fourteen other maxims, if you'd
ke to hear them."

"Only if you have one regarding honesty and open-
ess."

"I do. That would be my fourth maxim. Women be-
eve that keeping secrets adds to their mystery and al-
ire."

"I don't think Maddie considers her criminal record part of her allure."

"She's got a record?"

"She did, although it took a lot of digging to find i She spent some time in juvie. Petty crime, problems home. She was a pretty good pickpocket, according a few sources. From what I understand, she had rough childhood. She's been on her own since she wa twelve." Jack paused and smiled. "But you have know what she's accomplished to really appreciat Maddie Delaney. She's smart and clever and beaut ful. And she's tough...resilient. She doesn't let any thing stand in her way. She runs her own restaurant, real fancy place over in the Garden District."

"You sound like a man in love," Jeff teased.

"Well, maybe I am. Maybe I think that Maddie D laney is the only woman in the world for me."

Jeff shoved his chair back and stood up. "Come on, he said. "Let's go to your hotel and get you cleane up. Then you can find this Maddie Delaney and talk her. Maybe you can convince her that you're not suc a bad guy, after all."

Jack stared up at his brother for a long momen then sighed. Hell, he couldn't continue like this, hang ing out in bars and trying to drown his sorrows in never-ending supply of bourbon. He'd talk to Maddi lay his cards on the table. And if she didn't want any thing to do with him, he'd return to San Francisco. C maybe he'd even reenlist.

If there was one place he could forget Maddie D laney, it would be on an aircraft carrier out in the mi dle of the ocean. He was still a qualified frogman. Th navy would be lucky to get him back.

"All right," Jack finally said. "I'll go talk to her."

They walked back to Jack's hotel on Bourbon Stree

While Jack showered, Jeff called down for room service and ordered them both a decent breakfast of eggs, bacon, grits and biscuits. By the time Jack emerged from the shower, he felt like a new man, with only traces of the last few days evident in the dark circles under his eyes.

He wrapped himself in the robe that the hotel provided, then shaved off his three-day beard. "I'm too old for this," he muttered, drawing the razor over his cheek. "I used to be able to party with the best of them, but now it takes too much out of me."

He remembered back to all the furloughs he and Lucas Kincaid had spent together. They'd tried to outdo each other in everything—women, drinking, wild behavior. And they'd nearly ended up in the brig more times than he could count. Only fast talking, abject apologies—and their impeccable service record—had kept them out.

That life seemed so far away, part of a distant past. Yet that was who he had been—until he had come to Felicity. He could trace the change in his life to the moment he'd met Maddie. He was no longer the boy in a man's body. He wanted more than a life filled with balls-to-the-wall danger and hard partying.

There were certain things that required patience and humility to achieve. Falling in love with Maddie had taught him that. Just because he'd trained his sights on her didn't mean she was his. She wasn't like some target to be taken, some objective to be achieved.

She was a woman—a beautiful, desirable woman—who deserved a man who could love her with every fiber of his being. He could be that man. He could be there for Maddie, through the good times and the bad.

Jack grabbed the washcloth from the edge of the sink and wiped away the last traces of shaving cream.

"So this is one of the bad times," he said, meeting his own gaze in the mirror. "I've just got to turn things around here. Make her see that I'm the man for her."

When he stepped into the room, he found Jeff gorging himself on the just-delivered breakfast. Jack didn't realize how hungry he was until the smell of bacon wafted through the air. Jeff poured him a cup of coffee as he sat down and uncovered his plate.

"What's the plan?" Jeff asked.

"I'm going over to talk to her. The restaurant is open for lunch, so I know she'll be there."

"What if she doesn't want to talk to you?"

"She'll talk to me," Jack said.

"Still, you should have a contingency plan. I always have a contingency plan."

"That's the problem, Sparky. I've been approaching this thing the wrong way. The navy way. I just assumed if I pushed hard enough, then she'd be forced into an early surrender."

"Ah. Maxim number thirteen. Trying to make a woman do what you want her to do is like herding cats. They don't take direction well."

Jack munched on a warm biscuit drizzled with honey, then snatched up a piece of bacon. "The plan is to turn this back on her. Let her make all the choices."

"You're going to grovel?" Jeff asked.

"Groveling may be involved. As will a discussion of my feelings and an honest attempt at sensitivity."

"And if it doesn't work?"

Jack guzzled down his glass of orange juice, then wiped his mouth with his linen napkin. "I'm not willing to consider that possibility." He paused. "But if she slams the door in my face, I do have an alternate plan."

"Yeah?"

"Think they need a good frogman at Pensacola?"

Jeff grinned and bit off a good chunk of his biscuit. "Both of us on the same base? The navy would never be the same. For our country's sake, I hope she says yes."

They finished their breakfast, and while Jack got dressed, his brother made plans to see a little more of New Orleans. They agreed to hook up later at the hotel for what Jack hoped would be a celebration of sorts. He promised to bring Maddie along to meet his little brother. They parted in front of the hotel, Jeff heading toward Jackson Square and a tour of the Cabildo and Jack walking in the opposite direction, toward the St. Charles Avenue streetcar stop at the edge of the Quarter.

All the stops were familiar to him now, and he waited and got off at Washington Avenue, then strolled past Lafayette Cemetery to Magazine Street. As he walked, he tried to formulate a decent opening line. He wavered between demanding, apologetic and indifferent. Hell, maybe he ought to just pull her into his arms and kiss her. She always reacted quite enthusiastically to his kisses.

He'd reached Maddie's block before he'd made a decision. So he stood across the street in the doorway of an antique shop and stared at Delaney's. The woman he'd met that first day at the restaurant was hosing down the sidewalk and pulling weeds from the flower beds in front of the old town house.

He'd nearly decided to cross the street when the front door of the restaurant opened and Maddie stepped out. She looked so different, dressed in a starched white jacket and a chef's toque, her hair pulled back at her nape. She said a few words to the

woman, then walked back inside. A few moment
later, the woman followed.

Jack wasn't sure how long he stood watching th
front door of the restaurant, waiting for Maddie t
reappear. But when a group of businessmen climbe
the front steps and went inside, he glanced down a
his watch to see that it was noon. The restaurant wa
now open for business. "Damn," he muttered.

He could either go inside, or wait another two hour
until after the lunch crowd had left. He wasn't willin
to wait. Looking both ways, he crossed Magazin
Street and took the front steps of the restaurant two a
a time. The four businessmen were just being seated a
he stepped into the foyer.

When the hostess returned, she stepped behind th
ornately carved desk, then glanced up at him. He sav
a flicker of recognition in her eyes, then she smile
"Welcome back. I see you've decided to join us fo
lunch."

"Lunch," Jack said, nodding. "That sounds good."

Her eyebrow arched. "Do you have a reservation?"

"Do I need one?" Jack asked, glancing over at th
nearly empty dining room.

"Most of the tables are spoken for at lunch," sh
said.

Jack braced his palms on the desk and leaned closer
giving her his most charming grin. "I'm a friend of th
owner. Maddie Delaney?"

The woman cleared her throat and gave him a slow
once-over. "Just a moment," she said with a flirtatiou
smile. She disappeared through a door at the rear o
the foyer. Jack tugged at the knot in his tie and loos
ened the top button of his shirt. Jeff had lent him th
wardrobe, items his little brother had brought along i
case a wedding was in the works.

He adjusted the cuffs of his sport jacket and drew in a deep breath. This was it. This was for all the marbles. If he blew it now, there would be no going back. Jack closed his eyes and said a silent prayer, the same one he'd said before every dangerous engagement and tricky operation in the Gulf. Then he opened his eyes.

"*Hoo-ah*," he murmured halfheartedly. "Go, Navy."

"WHAT DO YOU MEAN, he's out there? Who?"

"Him!"

Maddie groaned. "The restaurant critic from the *Times-Picayune*? He was just here two months ago! He can't come today. We're all out of snapper and he always orders snapper."

"Not him!" Anne said. "John Q. Adonis. That hunk who was in here a few days back. The one you were running away from."

Maddie gasped. "Jack?" The spoon she held clattered to the floor, spattering hollandaise on her shoes. "Jack Beaumont is here? In *my* restaurant?"

"He wants lunch. I told him we're all booked, but he said he knew the owner. I got the distinct impression he meant in the biblical sense. Am I allowed to seat the former lover of the owner?"

Maddie gave her manager an aggravated glare. "Tell him to find someplace else to eat." Anne moved toward the door. "No! Wait," Maddie cried. She cursed softly. "Go ahead and seat him. Put him at the table in the morning room. And don't put anyone else in there."

"But that's—"

"I know it's Mr. Robillard's favorite spot. He won't complain as long as I whip him up a chocolate soufflé for dessert. He'd sit in the middle of Magazine Street for my chocolate soufflé."

Anne nodded, then left the kitchen. Maddie risked a look through the small window in the swinging door. She almost didn't recognize Jack. The jeans and chambray work shirt he usually wore had been replaced by a sports jacket and tie. It even looked like he'd used a comb, rather than his fingers, to style his hair.

As he turned toward the dining room, she caught a glimpse of his profile and her heart did a little flip in her chest. An image of him naked, sprawled in her bed, flashed in her mind, and a twinge of desire knotted in her stomach...until she remembered how she had left things.

The desire was quickly replaced by nagging nausea. She felt the pressure grow, weighing her down until she was barely able to breathe. Why had he come here? Was he going to press her about his marriage proposal? Would she be forced to explain herself?

The door swung inward, whacking her in the nose and Maddie cried out. Anne slowly pushed it open again and peered inside. "What are you doing? This is the In door!"

Maddie knew that! She'd carefully schooled every member of the wait staff on use of the two kitchen doors. In through the foyer door, out through the dining room door. It made for an easy flow through the restaurant and prevented accidental collisions with heavily loaded trays.

She rubbed her nose and scowled at Anne. "Did you seat him?"

Her manager nodded. "He's looking at the menu. Are you going to go talk to him?"

"Only if my nose doesn't swell up." She tipped her head. "Is it bleeding?"

Anne examined her. "Just a little red. Now get out there."

"I have meals to prepare," Maddie countered.

"Don't use that as an excuse. You've got two sous-chefs who ran this restaurant while you were gone. Let them cook while you talk."

Maddie took a deep breath and smoothed her hands over her jacket. "All right. I'm going to go say hello. Just hello. Like I do to all the customers. I'll be right back."

The tables were already beginning to fill with the lunch crowd as Maddie made her way out to the dining room. Several of her regulars stopped her and asked about the specials, and she was forced to chat for a while. The whole time she could feel Jack's eyes on her, and when she finally turned, he was there, staring across the room at her.

Maddie smiled hesitantly as she stepped up to his table. The room he sat in was at the rear of the dining room, in what used to be a small breakfast nook. It was lined with windows and overlooked Maddie's overgrown herb garden. It afforded the most privacy in the restaurant and held two of the most requested tables for four.

"Hello, Jack," she said, her voice cracking with nerves.

He fumbled with his menu. "Hi, Maddie."

"How did you find me?"

"I have my ways." He motioned to the seat across from him. "Sit down."

"I—I can't. I'm working."

"Maddie, please. We need to talk."

Reluctantly, she did as he asked. She carefully rearranged the antique silver flatware at her place setting, then straightened the crystal, before she folded her hands on top of the crisp linen tablecloth. "If you're here to discuss—"

"I'm here to find out why you walked out on me. I asked you to marry me, Maddie. I don't make marriage proposals lightly."

"I know," she said. "And I didn't take your proposal lightly."

"You never gave me an answer."

"I—I thought that—"

"What? That sneaking out in the middle of the night was a good enough answer? I think I deserve a direct reply, don't you?"

"Yes," she said.

"Yes, you'll marry me?"

"No!" Maddie cried. "I meant, yes, you deserve a reply. And...and my reply is no." She bit her bottom lip and sent him an apologetic smile. "It's no. I'm sorry, Jack, but I can't marry you."

"Is it because we haven't known each other for long?"

"Partly," she said.

"Then is it because you live here and I live in San Francisco? Hey, I really like Louisiana. I could be happy here."

"That's not the only problem."

He paused for a long moment, then met her gaze directly. "Is it because of your past?"

Maddie swallowed hard, her eyes going wide. "My past? What do you know about my past?"

Jack reached out to cover her hand with his, but she pulled away. "I know pretty much everything. How you lived on the streets for a while. How Lamar found you and took you in. How you didn't have much of a family life. Is that what it is, Maddie? Because all that makes no difference to me."

"How did you find out?" she said. "The records are sealed."

"I guessed part of it. And the rest wasn't too hard to figure out. What I didn't know, Lamar told me—after a rather heated phone call. I decided to call him a few days ago and force the issue. He filled in all the blanks."

Maddie tried to rise, but Jack caught her hand and pulled her back down. "That's all in the past, Maddie. I've got all sorts of skeletons in my closet. Navy SEALs don't exactly live a choirboy life. I've done things I wish I'd never had to do."

"It's different!" Maddie said.

"No, it's not. You said it before. You did what you had to do to survive. So have I. It's exactly the same."

She shook her head. How could he compare the two? Jack had served his country. Everything he'd done, he'd done in the name of honor and freedom. She had been a blight on society, stealing other people's hard-earned money, wasting taxes on her stays in juvie, taking up the social workers' time. "I've risen above my past," Maddie said.

"Yes, you have."

"And I've worked hard for everything I have. For Delaney's. For my life here in New Orleans. I'm used to being on my own. I've never wanted to be tied down in a relationship."

She knew the words would hurt him, would cut clear to the bone. But she could never admit she was afraid. Afraid that she might never live up to his expectations for a wife. Afraid that in the end he would discover his mistake and leave her.

As a kid on the street, she'd hidden her fears, using a false bravado to protect herself. And it came back now instinctively, when she needed protection from her own heart. She wanted so much to accept his proposal. To live happily ever after in his arms. She wanted the chance to become a good wife and a mother, to prove that she was worth loving. But there was always the fear, one that twisted her stomach into knots and hardened her heart. "I—I just thought we could have a good time together and leave it at that."

His expression grew cold. "I see. Well, I guess I can't offer any argument against that. After all, that's really what I was looking for, too. And we did have a good time, didn't we?"

Even though she knew his words were meant to hurt as much as hers did, she couldn't stop the dagger of pain from piercing her heart. It stole her breath away and brought hot tears to the corners of her eyes. She steeled herself and forced a smile. "I'm glad you understand," she said.

"Yeah," he said. "Right. I understand completely."

Maddie drew a deep breath. "So, I suppose you'll be going back to your job at the agency. You'll probably meet some gorgeous movie star and fall madly in love with her and forget all about me."

Jack shook his head. "Nah. I'm going to re-up in the navy. This civilian life is too sedate for me. I need some action, some danger in my life. Hell, I don't feel alive unless someone is shooting at me or trying to blow me up."

Maddie couldn't believe her ears. He couldn't mean to put his life in danger again! She remembered how she'd felt when he'd run out onto the gallery after Eulalie's first attempt on her life. And how she'd felt when he'd stood in the doorway of her bedroom, Eulalie's rifle pointed at his chest.

"But you're such a good bodyguard," she said. "You saved my life. Twice."

Jack nodded and smiled. "And now you're on your

wn. The way you like it." He placed his palms on the
ble then stood up. "Take care, Maddie."

He turned to walk out, but she jumped up and
ached out to stop him. "Wait."

Jack glanced down at her fingers, clutching the
eeve of his jacket. Then he looked at her. "Maddie,
ou'll be fine. In a few days, you'll hardly remember
e."

*No, I won't be fine*, she wanted to shout. *I will remem-
r you! Every night before I fall asleep. And every morning
hen I wake up.*

She wanted to hold on to him for just a little
nger—until she'd memorized every detail of his
ce, until she had taken her fill of his rich, deep voice.
ntil she'd convinced herself that she could let him
.

Maddie bit her bottom lip, then drew her trembling
and away. "I won't forget you, Jack Beaumont. I'll
ver forget you."

With that, she brushed by him, hurrying through
e dining room and into the kitchen. It was only
ere, after she'd closed herself inside her tiny office
ear the back door, that she allowed the tears to come.

Dammit, she would forget him. If it took her the rest
her natural born life, she'd learn to live without Jack
eaumont!

IADDIE STARED UP at the row house, tucked within a
ring of San Francisco's prettiest "painted ladies."
ouisiana boasted some of the country's most beauti-
l and unusual residential architecture—at Felicity,
r example, and in the French Quarter and the Gar-
en District of New Orleans. But she had to admit the
eadquarters for the S. J. Spade Agency had a certain

charm, with its view of the Golden Gate Bridge ar San Francisco Bay.

She paid the taxi driver, then hurried to the sid walk as she heard the sound of a streetcar bell. Sh was never sure where they were coming from or whe they'd appear. It would be just her luck to get fla tened by public transportation right after she'd final decided to work things out with Jack.

It hadn't taken long for her to change her min Barely a week had gone by and she had managed bury herself under a mountain of regret, aided by co stant phone calls and visits from Calpurnia and L mar.

They'd finally worn her down and made her s what she'd been too stubborn, too proud, to see. Sh wanted Jack, and she deserved him! They were mea: to be together, the two of them. The only thing stan( ing between them had been her misguided assum) tion that she could never let go of her past.

Well, she could let go and she would, starting nov She had let Jack Beaumont get away once, but sh wasn't going to let that happen again. She was here tell him exactly how she felt, and she intended to st; until he was quite clear about her change of heart.

As Maddie crossed the street and approached th front steps of the agency, a gorgeous blonde stro( purposefully down the sidewalk, her heels clickir against the concrete in a snappy rhythm. She balance a plate in her left hand, the contents hidden by tinfo She stopped where Maddie stood.

"Are you going up?" she asked, in a voice surpri ingly deep for a woman.

Maddie nodded.

"Then come on, honey." They climbed the lor flight of steps together and the blonde pushed ope the front door, then stepped aside to let Maddie pass. As she did, the woman sighed dramatically. "I just adore your hat. Ava Gardner wore one just like it in an old publicity shot I have of her."

"Thank you," Maddie said, touching the wide straw brim. She had chosen the hat carefully. And the stockings as well—taupe silk, with seams running up the back.

As they stood in the front hall, the woman held out her hand. "I'm Jon Wilcox."

Maddie blinked in surprise. The man was dressed in a gorgeous frock reminiscent of a dress Marilyn Monroe wore in *Gentleman Prefer Blondes*. In fact, with the beauty mark and the platinum blond hair, he looked eerily like the dead movie star. "You're— you're a man?"

Jon frowned, then laughed out loud, waving his hand. "Oh! Sometimes I forget how I'm dressed! Yes, there is a man underneath all this glamour. I usually don't go out as Marilyn during the day. But I've been to a rehearsal for a charity benefit and I wanted to drop off a little treat before I went back."

Maddie nodded, not sure what to say. What do you say to a man who looks better than you do in a dress and lipstick, even on your best day? A giggle of embarrassment bubbled up in her throat. "I—I'm sorry," she said, trying to cover. "I neglected to introduce myself. I'm—"

"You're the Black Widow!" Jon said.

"I'm what?"

"The widow that Beaumont was working for. I saw you the day you first came in. Oh, honey, I loved that suit. And that hat! I would die to own that hat you wore."

"Thank you," Maddie said.

"Mark told me that you own Delaney's in New Orleans. He read it in Beaumont's report. We ate there just last year. Mark and I went to Mardi Gras. You served an incredible oyster chowder and an exquisite roast duckling with sweet potatoes and honey and pecans. Oh, and for dessert there was an amaretto sabayon, the taste of which stays with me to this very day." He grabbed her hand and shook it. "It's such an honor to meet a chef of your caliber, Ms. Delaney."

"Why, thank you, Mr. Wilcox."

"Jon," he said. "Call me Jon." He drew her along with him. "Come, let's get you settled. Maybe after your appointment, you and I could get together and talk cooking. I hope to open my own restaurant very soon. I'm looking at properties right now. It's going to be a theme restaurant."

"And what is your theme?" Maddie asked.

He stopped and threw out his arms, then pointed to himself. "La Marilyn! The greatest movie star to ever live. I have tons of memorabilia that I'll put on display. I want to call the place Norma Jean's. Don't you think that has a wonderful ring to it?"

Maddie nodded, wondering if Jon Wilcox ever stopped to take a breath. "I look forward to eating there," she said.

Jon laughed again. "Listen to me, rattling on about myself when you've got an appointment."

"Actually, I don't have an appointment," Maddie said. "I was hoping I'd be able to see Jack."

Jon frowned, then tapped his crimson lips with a well-manicured fingertip. "I don't believe he's in. Come, let's go ask Mark."

Maddie followed "Marilyn" through the front hall, trying to imitate the easy sway of her hips as "she" walked. In just a few steps, she realized that as Jon

:epped, he put one foot directly in front of the other. Iaddie tested the technique and was pleased with the :minine allure it added to her gait.

Mark was seated in his office, the same richly ap- ointed room where she'd first met Jack. Warm wood aneling gave the office a formal look, and an ornate :replace, flanked by two tall, multipaned windows, ominated the far wall. The office, in keeping with the ictorian style, was filled with fussy, oversize furni- ire and fancy accessories.

She had to admit she preferred the antebellum sim- licity of Felicity more that this overblown style of de- or. The judge treated each antique in his house as if it ere a museum piece, giving it the proper space to be dmired.

Jon cleared his throat to get Mark's attention. "Hi, on! Look who I found on the front steps."

Mark jumped up from his chair and crossed the om. "Mrs. Parmen—I mean, Ms. Delaney. It's so ice to see you again." He held out his hand and she nook it. "What are you doing here in San Francisco?"

Maddie folded her hands in front of her, in part to op them from trembling with nerves. "I've come to e Mr. Beaumont," she said. "There are a few loose ids I need to tie up."

Mark frowned. "I hope there's no problem."

She shook her head. "Oh, no. Lamar got your final ll and everything was in order. He was quite pleased ith the service you provided and is happy to recom- iend you to any of his associates and friends."

"Good," Mark said, nodding. He glanced up at Jon, ien back at Maddie. "Well, Jack isn't in right now, it we expect him any minute. Can I get you some- ing to drink?"

"Let me take care of that," Jon offered. "I'll make

Ms. Delaney one of my famous café au laits. And the
she can taste test my newest little treat.''

Mark hesitated. ''Jon, I think—''

''Don't worry,'' Jon said. ''Ms. Delaney and I wi
settle ourselves in Jack's office and I'll keep her com
pany until he gets in. We have plenty to talk abou
don't we, Ms. Delaney?''

Maddie smiled at Jon, then nodded at Mark. ''Yes,
believe we do.''

As Jon promised, they waited in Jack's office, di
cussing all sorts of recipes and cooking technique
For a self-trained chef, Jon was quite well versed i
traditional French cooking techniques. They wer
deep in a discussion of pastry cream when they wer
interrupted.

''Maddie?''

Jon and Maddie twisted around in their chairs to se
Jack standing in the doorway. His hair was wind
blown and his color high, and his breath came in sho
gasps, as if he'd just run a mile or two to the office.

''Hello, Jack.''

''Well,'' Jon murmured. ''This diva knows when t
make her exit.'' He stood up, sent Jack a provocativ
smile and sashayed out of the room.

Jack shook his head. ''That guy. Always entertai
ing, I'll give him that.''

''He's awfully nice,'' Maddie said. ''He's going to b
a good chef someday. He has very unique and creativ
ideas about preparation and presentation. In fact, h
was just telling me about a recipe he has for...''

Jack slowly circled behind his desk and sat dow
''Maddie, you didn't come here to talk about cookin
did you?''

She twisted her fingers in her lap and shook h
head. Now that he was here, she wasn't sure what t

say. Since he'd left New Orleans, her days had been a drudgery and her nights a never-ending battle between insomnia and delicious dreams of him.

She had tried to forget Jack Beaumont. The problem was, it was ruining her life. The more she had tried to put him out of her head, the more she wanted him. Mistakes had been made, huge mistakes that might be irreversible. But she had to find out whether he could give her a chance to repair the mess she'd made of both her life and his.

"No," Maddie said. "I didn't come to talk about cooking. I came to see you."

"Why?"

"Have you reenlisted in the navy yet?" Maddie asked, knowing his answer would make or break her plan to get him back.

"What business is that of yours?"

His harsh tone made Maddie squirm in her seat. He was still mad, bitter even. She didn't blame him. She'd treated him horribly. "It is my business," she said. "I need a bodyguard, so I came to you."

A look of concern crossed his handsome features. "Is everything all right? They didn't let Eulalie out of the psychiatric ward, did they?"

"No. I don't actually need protection. You see, this bodyguard has to provide a very special type of…service."

"And what might that be?"

She drew a deep breath, knowing that the next few minutes would determine the course of the rest of her life. "Well, first of all, I need a man who will be available twenty-four hours a day. A man who will share my days and nights, someone who will comfort me when I'm upset and laugh with me when I'm happy."

Jack's expression softened and a smile quirked the

corners of his lips. "Sounds like a very interesting job."

"I'm looking for someone who is kind and patient. Understanding. A bodyguard who will accept me for who I am. A man who will put up with my stubbornness and my independence."

He leaned back in his chair and laced his fingers together behind his head. "And what would be the compensation package for this bodyguard?"

"Well," Maddie said. "Room and board would be provided. Of course, the food will be extraordinary, although the living quarters might be a little cramped. But we could work that out. I don't have to mention that you would be spending all your time with me, a situation to which many men have aspired."

"Many?" Jack said.

Maddie smiled. "Well, maybe that was a slight exaggeration. All right, a few."

"A few?"

"Yes," Maddie said. "A few. They've aspired but they've never achieved."

"Ah," Jack said. "So, I would be the first bodyguard to occupy this special position in your life."

"Yes."

"Well, Ms. Delaney, I think I could do the job."

Maddie's heart leaped. She had been right to come! They still had a future together. "You could?"

"But I'm not sure about the compensation package," he said, leaning forward in his chair. "There are several other things I require in the way of payment."

"What would those be?" Maddie asked.

He slowly stood and rounded his desk, then pulled her up out of her chair. Gently, he placed his fingertips on her lips. "Unlimited kisses," he said. His mouth brushed against hers, fleeting, tempting.

"Done," Maddie replied.

He bent close to her ear. "Sweet words of passion. very day."

"Done," she whispered in his ear. She followed ith a lurid suggestion that caused him to chuckle nd wrap his arm around her waist.

"But most of all," he said. "I want this." Jack placed is fingertips below her collarbone. "I want your eart, Maddie."

Tears pushed at the corners of her eyes and she gave im a wavering smile. "Done," she murmured. She linked, then brushed a tear from her cheek. "Will you sk me again?"

Jack put on a confused scowl. "Ask you what?"

Maddie slapped his chest playfully. "You know! sk me again."

"Oh, right. The question. Now what was it?"

Maddie narrowed her eyes and twisted the front of is shirt up to his chin.

"All right, all right! Madeline Delaney, will you arry me?"

"Yes!" Maddie cried, throwing herself into his ms. "Yes, Jack Beaumont, I will marry you."

He kissed her, long, slowly and deeply, until her es and her fingertips went numb. And when she ought she couldn't take any more, he lifted her off er feet and kissed her again.

"I love you, Maddie," he murmured against her outh.

"And I love you, Jack."

He turned her around and lifted her up onto the lge of his desk, sliding her skirt up along her thighs nd stepping between her legs. His hands skimmed ver her body as his mouth plundered hers. Then he

cupped her face in his hands and stepped back to ga:
down into her eyes. "God, I've missed you," he said

As her thoughts slowly came back into focus, Ma
die's heart lurched. "You didn't answer my question
she said, a desperate edge to her voice.

"What question was that?"

"Did you reenlist in the Navy?"

Jack grinned. "Would you still marry me if I did?"

Maddie frowned, her hands toying with the buttor
of his shirt. "Of course I'd still marry you. But we'd l
apart for so long and I'd miss you so much and I—"

Jack pressed his finger over her lips. "I didn't r
enlist."

Maddie wrapped her arms around his neck ar
pulled him down until their noses pressed again
each other's. "Then you'll promise to guard my boc
day and night, for better or for worse, in sickness ar
in health, forsaking all others, till death do us part?"

"And I'll wash dishes in your restaurant and scru
your back in the shower and bring you breakfast
bed every Sunday morning." Jack growled, then nu
zled her neck, sending a sweet shudder of desi
coursing through her body. "Because, sweetheart, I'
your man."

Don't miss Temptation's next...

HERO FOR HIRE

## #701 IN HOT PURSUIT

by

PATRICIA RYAN

Of all the bodyguard assignments
Roman Fitzpatrick had endured, this one was
the hardest. He'd been hired to protect
Summer Love; she didn't want to be protected.
He blamed gossip-hungry, irresponsible
journalists for destroying his police career; she
was a flighty gossip columnist. He was a man;
she was a woman....

Available in October

Here's a preview!

"I THOUGHT YOU SAID *bodyguards weren't supposed to be confrontational*."

Summer held Roman's gaze steadily, but her voice had a breathy quality he hadn't heard before.

He found himself leaning closer to her. "There's just so much provocation I can ignore before instinct takes over and I just act."

"What do you know," she said with that drowsy-eye smile that made his blood pound in his veins. "Scratch the surface of Eliot Ness and you find a caveman underneath."

"Maybe you should stop scratching," he suggested in a low, almost threatening voice.

"Maybe." She smiled, her gaze unflinching. "But I always kind of had a thing for Fred Flintstone."

She uncrossed her arms and placed her hands against his chest. Roman's mind spun dizzily, wondering what was coming next, but she merely pushed him back and ducked under his right arm. "So, from here on out, it seems you've got me on your little leash. I'll sit, stay, roll over...Just give the command."

"Is that your way of saying you're going to cooperate with me?"

She sighed and raked her fingers through her hair. "I *am* trying to cooperate, but I can't possibly avoid large gatherings. I make my living going to parties and writing about them—important parties given by important people."

Roman scrubbed at his chin. "All right, go to the parties, but don't go anywhere without me."

"See, now, there's another problem. Somehow I just can't see either Fred Flintstone *or* Eliot Ness fitting into the San Francisco social scene. How am I supposed to introduce you?"

"Say you got me from the Goon of the Month Club."

A smile tugged at her lips. "Another joke. You may be human after all." She tilted her head and appraised him with such intense concentration that his skin tingled. "I sometimes bring dates to these things. You want to be my boyfriend? We'll make you lead guitarist for a rock band. Everyone knows I've got a weakness for guitarists."

"Got a pretty active social life, do you? I've got this mental image of you juggling men like oranges."

"It's too easy to drop them that way, and then they end up bruised. I try to keep just one orange in the air at any given time."

"How bourgeois of you."

"It's not real monogamy, more like…serial monogamy."

"Hunk of the Month Club?"

"That's right, and you've just been elected Mr. September." She cocked an eyebrow. "Think Eliot can handle the likes of me?"

"No." Roman allowed himself a devilish smile. "But Fred probably can."

# Take 2 bestselling love stories FREE

## Plus get a FREE surprise gift!

## Special Limited-Time Offer

### Mail to Harlequin Reader Service®

P.O. Box 609
Fort Erie, Ontario
L2A 5X3

**YES!** Please send me 2 free Harlequin Temptation® novels and my free surprise gift. Then send me 4 brand-new novels every month, which I will receive before they appear in bookstores. Bill me at the low price of $3.57 each plus 25¢ delivery and GST.* That's the complete price, and a saving of over 10% off the cover prices—quite a bargain! I understand that accepting the books and gift places me under no obligation ever to buy any books. I can always return a shipment and cancel at any time. Even if I never buy another book from Harlequin, the 2 free books and the surprise gift are mine to keep forever.

342 HEN CH7H

| Name | (PLEASE PRINT) | |
|---|---|---|
| Address | Apt. No. | |
| City | Province | Postal Code |

This offer is limited to one order per household and not valid to present Harlequin Temptation® subscribers. *Terms and prices are subject to change without notice. Canadian residents will be charged applicable provincial taxes and GST.

CTEMP-98

©1990 Harlequin Enterprises Limited

# HARLEQUIN®
## *Temptation*

*He's strong. He's sexy.
He's up for grabs!*

Harlequin Temptation and
*Texas Men* magazine present:

### *1998 Mail Order Men*

**#691 THE LONE WOLF**
by Sandy Steen—July 1998

**#695 SINGLE IN THE SADDLE**
by Vicki Lewis Thompson—August 1998

**#699 SINGLE SHERIFF SEEKS...**
by Jo Leigh—September 1998

**#703 STILL HITCHED, COWBOY**
by Leandra Logan—October 1998

**#707 TALL, DARK AND RECKLESS**
by Lyn Ellis—November 1998

**#711 MR. DECEMBER**
by Heather MacAllister—December 1998

*Mail Order Men—
Satisfaction Guaranteed!*

Available wherever Harlequin books are sold.

# HARLEQUIN®
*Makes any time special* ™

Look us up on-line at: http://www.romance.net          HTEMOM

# MEN at WORK

## All work and no play?
## Not these men!

**July 1998**

### MACKENZIE'S LADY by Dallas Schulze

Undercover agent Mackenzie Donahue's
lazy smile and deep blue eyes were his best
weapons. But after rescuing—and kissing!—
damsel in distress Holly Reynolds, how could
he betray her by spying on her brother?

**August 1998**

### MISS LIZ'S PASSION by Sherryl Woods

Todd Lewis could put up a building with ease,
but quailed at the sight of a classroom! Still,
Liz Gentry, his son's teacher, was no battle-ax,
and soon Todd started planning some
extracurricular activities of his own....

**September 1998**

### A CLASSIC ENCOUNTER
### by Emilie Richards

Doctor Chris Matthews was intelligent, sexy
and *very* good with his hands—which made
him all the more dangerous to single mom
Lizette St. Hilaire. So how long could she
resist Chris's special brand of TLC?

Available at your favorite retail outlet!

## MEN AT WORK™

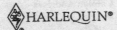 

Look us up on-line at: http://www.romance.net

PMAW2

# Temptation®

## COMING NEXT MONTH

**#701 IN HOT PURSUIT Patricia Ryan**
Hero for Hire

Of all the bodyguard assignments Roman Fitzpatrick had endured, this was the hardest. He had to protect Summer Love; she didn't want protection. He blamed gossip-hungry journalists for destroying his police career; she was a flighty gossip columnist. He was a man; she was a woman....

**#702 LOVE YOU FOREVER Janice Kaiser**
The Cowboy Club

The moment Erica Ross walked into the Cowboy Club her life changed. The legendary Western place oozed romance and cowboys. And tall, sexy, strapping Clay McCormick was exactly the kind of man she needed. But could it last *forever*?

**#703 STILL HITCHED, COWBOY Leandra Logan**
Mail Order Men

Matt Colter advertised for the woman of his dreams in *Texas Men* magazine. What he got was a nightmare! A blond socialite fiancée, Tiffany—and a beautiful brunette ex-wife, Jenna, who wasn't *exactly* an ex. This cowboy was still hitched, still in love...and he had to follow his heart!

**#704 A TOUCH OF BLACK VELVET Carrie Alexander**
Blaze

Alec Danielli *knew* that being Lacey Longwood's protector would sorely test him. She was the Black Velvet vixen, Madame X—*every* man's fantasy. And he couldn't touch her....

## AVAILABLE NOW: